PENGUIN BOOKS

THE END OF A FAMILY STORY

The great Hungarian writer Péter Nádas has become known in the past decade as one of the most important literary voices of Central Europe. Mr. Nádas was born in Budapest in 1942. Though he has said that he always wanted to be a writer, his first professional work was as a news photographer, work that he continued until the events of the "Prague Spring" of 1968. His first published fiction appeared in the 1960s; *The End of a Family* Story was published in Hungary in 1977; his second novel, *A Book of Memories*, in 1986. A novelist, playwright, and essayist whose work has been accorded great tribute and recognition internationally, Nádas continues to live and work in Gombosszeg, Hungary.

Also by Péter Nádas

A Book of Memories

PENGUIN BOOKS
Published by the Penguin Group
Penguin Putnam Inc., 375 Hudson Street,
New York, New York 10014, U.S.A.
Penguin Books Ltd, 27 Wrights Lane, London W8 5TZ, England
Penguin Books Australia Ltd, Ringwood, Victoria, Australia
Penguin Books Canada Ltd, 10 Alcorn Avenue,
Toronto, Ontario, Canada M4V 3B2
Penguin Books (N.Z.) Ltd, 182–190 Wairau Road,
Auckland 10, New Zealand

Penguin Books Ltd, Registered Offices:
Harmondsworth, Middlesex, England

First published in the United States of America by
Farrar, Straus and Giroux 1998
Published in Penguin Books 2000

1 3 5 7 9 10 8 6 4 2

Originally published in 1977 by Szépirodalmi Könyvkiadó,
Budapest, Hungary, as *Egy családregény vége*

PUBLISHER'S NOTE

This is a work of fiction. Names, characters, places, and incidents are either the product of the author's imagination or are used fictitiously, and any resemblance to actual persons, living or dead, business establishments, events, or locales is entirely coincidental.

THE LIBRARY OF CONGRESS HAS CATALOGED
THE AMERICAN HARDCOVER EDITION AS FOLLOWS:
Nádas, Péter, 1942–
[Családregény története. English]
The end of a family story: a novel/ by Péter Nádas;
translated from the Hungarian by Imre Goldstein.
p. cm.
ISBN 0-374-14832-5 (hc.)
ISBN 0 14 02.9179 2 (pbk.)
I. Goldshtain, Imri, 1938– . II. Title.
PH3291.N297C7313 1998
894'.511334—dc21 98-7887

Printed in the United States of America
Set in Sabon
Designed by Jonathan Lippincott

The End of a Family Story

A Novel by

Péter Nádas

Translated from the Hungarian by

Imre Goldstein

PENGUIN BOOKS

And the light shineth in the darkness; and the darkness comprehended it not.

—John 1:5

The End of a Family Story

Among lilacs and hazel bushes, under the elderberries. Not far from that tree where sometimes a leaf would stir even with no wind blowing. We three were the family: papa, mama, and the child. I was the Papa, Éva the Mama. In the bushes it was always evening. "Always go to sleep! Why do I always have to go to sleep?" Mama has already tucked in the child. "Papa, tell the child a story!" She was banging the pots while she did the dishes in the kitchen. I was sitting at my desk, pretending to be studying Russian from Nina Potapova's reader, but when she said that to me I got up and went into the nursery. We had lined this room with hay to make it nice and soft. I sat down at the edge of the bed and drew the child's head onto my lap. I could dig my fingers into his wet hair; I hugged him. As if my own mother were hugging me. I could flatten my palm against his clammy forehead and wouldn't know whether it was my own palm I felt or his forehead. A thick vein was bulging out on his neck. If I cut that vein, all his blood would flow out. In the kitchen Mama was always making a racket with the pots. "Hurry up with that story, Papa, we'll be late for the party!" She was always in a hurry to go to some party, but I did not rush with the story because it felt good sitting there like that, with the child's wet head on my lap. "What story should I tell you?" The child opened his eyes. "I'd like to hear about the tree again." The way he looked at me made me think not of the story but of how good it would be if he really were my child, lying like this on my lap. "Very well, then, I'll tell you about the tree; close your eyes and listen. Once upon a time there was a tree. This special tree had a leaf. Of course it had thousands of leaves, but the one I'm telling you about was a very special leaf, not like the others. The tree in my story stood in a haunted garden. Nobody really knew this garden, people only knew that somewhere there was such a garden. But search as they might, they couldn't find it. And there were plenty of searchers, too. They even used those sniffing police dogs. Stop fidgeting! From the street the garden couldn't be seen. Not even from an airplane. But we knew how to get in. Behind a bush was the entrance to the secret tunnel. Through the tunnel, from the street, straight into the garden! Bats lived in this secret tunnel. They were there to protect the garden. Bats have stinking bodies. But we went anyway, because I knew all I had to do was yell, Fly away, bats, don't come back or I'll stick you in my sack! That made the bats hide in the darkest corners of the tunnel. Because we also took along a flashlight, a good strong one. But the passage was still not clear, because that's when the octopuses came. They had eyes like spotlights, made of reflectors. If someone strayed into the tunnel, right away they started swimming toward him. These are amphibious octopuses that can swim very fast in the air, too. At night they come out of their caves, but then they don't use their eyes, because they don't want to be seen. Anyway, if somebody wanders in there, zoom! they get him, they wrap themselves around him, hug him tight, and twist him until they've squeezed the last bit of life out of him. As we were walking we noticed that the floor of the cave was strewn with bones. Because lots of people wandered into the cave, but none of them ever reached the garden. This we hadn't figured in our plans. We thought that once we got past the bats the passage would be clear." Grandmama lay in bed all day sucking on sourballs. They had a filling, these sourballs, and she bought them for 2.40 in the supermarket. I too liked this kind of sourball a lot, because I could suck on it for a while, sliding it back and forth inside my mouth, rolling it around with my tongue; and then suddenly I'd bite down and all the raspberry-flavored filling would gush out. Grandmama always went by herself to buy the sourballs. She'd buy six times a hundred grams. One packet for every day of the week except Fridays, when she fasted. She put the paper packets under her pillow. The sourballs would melt under the pillow, stick to one another and to the paper bag. If she told me I could have one, sometimes I'd manage to tear out as many as three at a shot. But sometimes she'd give me none. "Grandmama, give me some candy!" "No!" "Grandmama, give me some candy!" "Haven't got any." "Grandmama, don't lie to me!" "I'm telling you I haven't got any, and even if I did I wouldn't give you any. Candy ruins your teeth. You mustn't ruin your teeth. Teeth are important to your health!" She was lying on the bed, wearing all black because Grandpapa had died. Since Grandpapa's death Grandmama had stopped cooking. I ate bread spread with fat or mustard, and she kept chewing her candy. But at night she didn't sleep, she'd stand by the window because she said that Grandpapa was coming home but one didn't know when he'd arrive. Grandpapa used to tell me lots of stories. But not fairy tales, real stories. "Now I will tell you about the happy times of my life." And then he would tell me about all those happy times. Or he would say, "Now I will tell you how I escaped from the jaws of death. Once, on the third of January, 1915, we went on a patrol with my hussars. There was a great fog all over Serbia that day. As we were riding, I heard some strange hoofbeats. I thought to myself it was our own horses with the thick fog doubling the sound of their hooves. Then in a few seconds strange riders emerged from the fog. They were like shadows, but there was no time to think. We were so close to them that if horses weren't smarter than people we would have collided. The horses were rearing up and neighing. And that damn Serb had already drawn his sword! So I drew mine! We clashed. But he had the advantage because he was above me, standing on higher ground. I stab, he slashes—and if I hadn't crouched, making myself small in the saddle, my head would have flown right off. As it was, he only got my hat. Well, I said to myself, it's all over for me. But then one of my hussars was suddenly on the spot. By the time that damn Serb could raise his sword again to bring it down from above—he could have sliced me and my horse right in half!—my hussar had chopped off his head." Grandpapa laughed so hard when he told me this story, his denture fell out, loose in his mouth. Always he'd manage to shove it neatly back in place. "That was my first great escape. Or maybe my birth saved me. God did come to my rescue. In Fiume it was, right on my birthday. In the fall of 1916, on the tenth of November, exactly. The flagship *Prinz Eugen* was in front, we were following behind. Barely out of port an hour when suddenly a shot was fired, bang! The *Prinz Eugen* sprang two leaks and promptly sank. All hands were lost, drowned at sea. We continued safely on our way and docked in Durrësi. But all this time I had an ugly abscess in my armpit, so bad I couldn't lower my arm. And when we landed a cholera epidemic was waiting for us, everybody got it, but I survived that, too. And in Fiume I'd wanted to get on the *Prinz Eugen*. Imagine. Because of that abscess I couldn't have swum even if I'd had the chance! Well, God wouldn't let me die, He helped me. You can see for yourself, here I am. Eighty-four years old. Pretty long time! But after that so many other things happened. From the fifth floor somebody threw a fancy candlestick out. We had been driven hard for the third day, and I wasn't very young, either. It was a forced march because the Russians were hard on our heels. We were lucky if they gave us a break, maybe twice a day. But there was no time even to take a shit. When we stopped we all just dropped. Once, I was lying on the ground, it was in the woods of Saalfeld, and I'm looking at the ground, I'd been there before, in my youth—but for such different reasons!—and I'm thinking how nice and soft it is here. So right to take me back; after all, hadn't I come back to it, to this same spot? This is where I stay, my place is here, inside you, I'm thinking, from this place I must not get up again, I'm thinking." Grandpapa always raised his head when he got to this point in the story and yelled so hard that his mouth turned black: "*Aufstehen! Schnell! Los! Schnell! Los!*" He'd pause a long time, his paleness slowly coming back. "And I'm thinking as I lie on the ground, Go ahead, yell, you can yell all you want, for all I care. I've already returned myself to Mother Earth. You see, that's the kind of vain animal man is. Believes he's in control of his own life. As if his life were a function of his own will. My, how wrong you can be! It didn't matter what I was thinking, everything turned out differently. This German stops over me. *Warum stehst du nicht auf, mein lieber Jude?* With some effort I look up at him. I see he's already drawn his pistol. Well then, this is the end. But what I wanted, what I wanted was that it should happen my way, according to my will, not his. Will you please shoot me! But he didn't. He replaced his pistol. He looked at me. He had wise brown eyes, like a dog's. He spat on me. And then gave me a good hard kick and went on his way. That's how God saved my life. Left me there on the road, so I could live." After Grandpapa died, Grandmama would turn off all the lights, sit down on my bed to tell me stories. She didn't like to waste electricity. Once I asked her to tell me a story about my mother. But she waited until I fell asleep. I preferred made-up stories. When I played the Papa and we put the child to bed, I always made up a story. The story about the tree continued with our getting hold of two sticks. "And those octopuses came at us! A hundred of 'em! Each octopus had fifty tentacles. I was whacking away! They saw they couldn't do anything to us! And in a jiffy, we were in the garden! All they could do was look at our backs! But then we had an eyeful, too! Because this garden was full of trees. Very special trees! Trees of every kind, but we couldn't tell just what kind. The one we thought was a peach tree had plums hanging from it, along with cherries, sour cherries, and even bunches of grapes. We could eat to our heart's content. But the tree I want to tell you about we only noticed later." But I didn't go on with the story. A strange head was asleep on my lap. I didn't know myself how I'd gotten here. Through a half-open mouth it was breathing evenly. Somewhere, far away, a car stopped, but the engine kept idling. It was as if I saw myself sleeping in my own lap. It would have felt so good to lower my head next to his, to sleep alongside him. Carefully I lifted my hand from his forehead. He felt it, stirred a little, and closed his mouth. Now he was breathing noisily through his nose. The engine of the car was purring out on the street. I'd have liked to have a forehead like his, but on mine the hair grew from lower down, and I was ashamed of that. Éva was still scrubbing the pots in the kitchen. The heat seemed stuck, there was no breeze to move it. Though the spots of light were quivering, their rhythm was unpredictable. One tiny spot was moving on his forehead, lit a trail into his hair, then vanished. I was sorry I'd taken my hand away. I would have liked to feel again that my hand was his forehead. "Why aren't you telling him the story?" "He's asleep. Not pretending, he's really fallen asleep." Éva put the pot on the shelf. The shelf is a piece of wood between two branches, but we call it the kitchen cabinet. If we kicked the branches, the pots, full of holes, fell to the ground. Then Éva would always say, "Papa, the kitchen cabinet fell apart, it's really time you fixed it!" But this time the pots didn't fall down, though when she slipped in next to me and tried to be careful, she did kick the bush. I could smell her. It seemed as if not the light but her skin was quivering. "We have to get to the party!" She was wearing tiny bathing shorts and a bra with frills. No matter how much she pulled and tugged at her breasts, they hadn't grown large enough to fill the bra. For the party we would always crawl out from under the bushes, her pink tulle outfit reaching to the ground, and she'd say she was also wearing jewelry. "One mustn't wear too much. A woman should wear only a few pieces, but they should be expensive and chosen carefully, you understand?" Everyone would be watching her. When she danced she would gently raise her long skirt, holding it gingerly with two fingers. "The chandeliers are lit! Crystal chandeliers!" But I didn't feel like crawling out to the party. Now I could feel the touch and weight of both bodies at once. "Let's make love instead!" And I took her in my arms. I felt her smell in my mouth, the same smell that came from the drying hair of the child and the one that also lingered in their house. "How?" I fell back, her body fell with me. Now I have to kiss her, now I have to kiss her. "Like this." Her naked belly on mine. The child's warm head on my groin. But somewhere up in the garden their mother began to yell: "Gáboréva, out of the water! Gáboréva, out of the water! Gáboréva, out of the water!" Because she thought we were still in the pool. Éva bit into my neck. We were looking at each other. I rubbed the spot where she bit me, even though I didn't want to and it didn't even hurt. Their mother was standing on the terrace, wearing the dressing gown she'd once taken off. And naked she'd crossed the room we were playing in. In vain I waited for her to do that again. It was odd that whenever I waited for something to happen it never did. Sometimes we also played that I was the child, and then Gábor would be the Papa. What made that interesting was that he behaved very differently. But after supper, when they put me to bed, he also told stories. When they played at making love I had to close my eyes. Éva said that

Gábor really knew how to kiss. And sometimes we played that I was the Papa and Gábor the Mama. Éva would always snuggle up to her Mama. She didn't like her Papa because he didn't come home from Argentina. When I was the child it was good, because she was the Mama. When Gábor played the Papa he traveled to Argentina. My father came home rarely. We always knew when, because he'd send a telegram to let us know. I'd be on the lookout for him, on the street. When I saw him I'd run toward him. I'd run and he'd be walking, carrying his brown briefcase. He'd spread his arms only when we were very close. His face was stubbly because he always had to travel at night. And his clothes stank because he lived in the barracks where they held those interrogations. But I did like this smell. I clung to him with my arms around his neck and he kept on walking like that. Then he'd pry my arms from around his neck and stick his cap on my head. When he thought I wouldn't notice, he'd look at me as if he didn't like me. But I did notice. He drew his finger across my mouth. His cap stank, too. Grandmama cleaned his fatigue jacket, his pants, and even his cap—in benzene, so they'd dry faster. And he'd leave again on the morning train. While he was at home nobody was allowed to smoke so we wouldn't blow up. He would sit in Grandpapa's armchair, wearing Grandpapa's housecoat. No matter which way I looked at him, he wasn't at all like

Grandpapa. I thought that if he hadn't turned out like Grandpapa, then I wouldn't turn out like him. I was usually still asleep when he had to go, but he'd come over and kiss me and draw his finger across my mouth. His face then would be smooth, only his clothes would smell of benzene. Whenever Grandpapa started to talk he would always yell. When he wasn't talking, he would clasp his hands, slip them between his knees, let his head droop, his shoulders would sag, and it was hard to see how big he was. And if he couldn't talk to anybody for a long time, he'd fall asleep in the armchair. Father crossed his legs when he sat; with one elbow he'd lean on his knee, hold his cigarette in his other hand, then suddenly he'd jump up and begin pacing around the room. He kept lifting things and looking at them as if seeing them for the first time. He would smell the food. And he'd also draw his fingers across the furniture. And when he had had enough of walking about, he'd lie down on the bed; I could tell he would have liked to sleep, he even closed his eyes, but then he'd look up and for no reason at all burst out laughing. "Why are you laughing?" He'd wrinkle his forehead. "I'm laughing? No, I'm not. It's nothing. Maybe I thought of something amusing." Sometimes I'd try to see what happened when I laughed. So I'd laugh, but he wouldn't ask me why. If he had, I would have told him that I laughed to see how he felt when he laughed. In the evening I was allowed to lie next to him in his bed and I'd ask him to tell me a story. "A story? Let's see now! I swear I can't think of a single story, nothing. Wait! Should I tell you about the boots? All right. Once upon a time, way beyond the seven seas, there were two boots. They were a real pair. And they were friends. Such good friends that nobody could imagine one without the other. Whenever one took a step, so did the other. When the other stopped, the one did, too. That's why one boot was called One and the other was called Other. And One and Other were together not only during the day but at night, too. Every night they stood at the foot of the bed. They liked to sleep like that, standing up. They didn't get very tired, because they leaned on each other. They both liked to feel the skin of the other. Actually they had no other wish than to stay like that. That's how they lived their lives. But slowly they grew old. They were thrown out, on the garbage heap. One was thrown to the right, the other to the left. And then—and then I don't know what happened. That's the end of the story. Go to sleep now." But I didn't want to believe that was the end of it. However, I had to go back to my own bed. "And the boots, whatever happened to the boots?" I asked him when he came home again and I was lying next to him in the dark. "What boots?" "The boots that were friends." "Oh, the boots! I don't know, I've no idea what happened to them." When he left on the morning train I thought how good it would be if I could be like him. Or if I could be like Grandpapa. But I couldn't make up my mind, because I also thought that it might be good to be like Gábor's and Éva's mother, who walked naked across the room and wasn't ashamed at all. If she'd been my mother I could have had a forehead like Gábor's. When Gábor was the Papa, and Mama had already tucked me in, he would come over to my bed in the nursery. He didn't take my head into his lap, but he put both his palms on my neck. Sometimes he would squeeze it a little as if to choke me, and then we would have a fight. But when he didn't squeeze my neck he would tell me stories. He liked to tell me about the woman whose name was Cleopatra and her picture was in one of their books. "Once, a woman whose name was Cleopatra was lying in her room and it was terribly hot. You want me to beat you up? She was lying in bed in her room. As she is lying there the door opens, just like that. But nobody comes in. Who is it? asked the woman. Maybe ghosts. But then she saw it wasn't a ghost who opened the door but a serpent. What do you want, serpent? asked the woman called Cleopatra. I've come to be at your service, hissed the serpent. That's nice of you, the broad says, but I've already got servants, a hundred of them! You'll never find a servant like me! How so, what can you do, serpent, asks the dame." "Don't tell it like that, call her by her real name!" "Shut up! So the chick asks what the serpent can do that her servants can't. And the serpent just laughs. You're suffering from the heat, aren't you, Cleopatra? Of course I am. And your servants can't help you, can they? Of course they can't. I am cold as ice! says the serpent. I'll climb on you and cool off your body. Come on, then! said the woman. The serpent slithered onto her body, across her belly, all the way up to her titties, took a good look at everything. And while doing it, the serpent asked Cleopatra, Would you like an apple? Oh, I'm still so hot, no, I don't want to eat now. Don't go away! Keep sliding all over me because you're really so nice and cold. Well, that's all the serpent needed to hear, it kept sliding and slithering all over Cleopatra until finally it slipped into her hole. But it couldn't crawl out. So it just settled in, kept on living there, which was good for Cleopatra, too, because she wasn't hot anymore. Only her belly started to swell, because she thought she was going to have a baby. They cut up her belly, and then the serpent came out with all the little serpents, because it wasn't Cleopatra that gave birth to the young ones but the clever serpent. And wicked Cleopatra died." I listened to the whole thing, even though I knew the ending of the story, and also knew that when he got to the end I'd start a fight with him. "That's so stupid, and it's not even true!" But we also fought when I told him the story about the tree. Because that story went on with us eating ourselves silly with all that fruit, then lying down on the grass. "Our stomachs were so full we couldn't even close our eyes. As we are lying there we notice a tree branch bending over us; the tree was like all the other trees and the branch was like all the other branches. Still, at the tip of this branch was one leaf that was very special. It would stir as if it were nodding. As if it were saying something we couldn't understand. None of the other leaves moved, just this one. Then it too stopped moving. We got scared, 'cause this must have meant something, and what would happen if we didn't understand what the leaf said? Then it moved again. But not like before; not like this but like that, as if this time it didn't want something to happen, I mean it wasn't nodding like before. The other leaves didn't move at all. Leaves have a special language, but you can learn it only with a magic drink. Then the leaf spoke to us for the third time. It started out slowly, got faster, then slowed down, got very slow, to be sure we understood it. But we didn't. We'd better get out of here and look for that magic drink. If we had understood the leaf we could have stayed in the garden until the day we died." He opened his eyes. I thought we'd start fighting. "There is no such garden, and leaves can't talk!" "Yes, they can!" If he started the fight, I wouldn't try to stop him. He could beat me as much as he wanted to. Even if I started the fight he would win. But I still didn't like the stories he told me about the woman. The apartment was in our garden, but we cut a hole in the fence so we could crawl in from their garden, too. When they wouldn't come, I'd just wait for them. The crack between the bushes we called the window. They'd swim in the pool. Go for a boat ride in the tub. They'd go up to the terrace from which their mother used to yell, wearing that dressing gown. They'd play ball. But I couldn't spy on them for too long because they were also peeking to see if I was there. Then I'd go into the house. I was alone. I knew, today they won't come. I can do anything I want to with the apartment. I could turn it upside down. But I didn't do anything. Whenever I waited for something to happen and it didn't, I got frightened. I was afraid that it would always be like this. Grandpapa lay in bed for two whole days before they took him away. He lay in the same position, all the time. Didn't even notice if a fly landed on his eyes. Grandmama slept during the day. I stood there looking at him, listening, trying to hear whether he was breathing. Whenever I remembered that he'd died, I'd run home. Grandmama didn't always lie on her bed. When she left the house she'd get dressed. She'd put on her silk dress with the big flowers. She'd throw the black dress she wore in bed on Grandpapa's armchair. And her white hat and white pocketbook lay there on the table. "Don't you go anywhere! They called me over to their place. As a witness!" She put on her white hat and looked at herself in the mirror. It was no use asking her to take me with her. She said it was something very serious and she had a very important job to do. A secret one. I already knew that my head could pass through between the iron bars. It didn't matter that she locked the door. On the terrace where their mother in her dressing gown used to yell, two men were standing. Smoking cigarettes. The tub was floating in the pool. Our game was to pull the plug, let the ship sink, and then the pirates won. I saw Grandmama's hat bobbing past the stair banister. One of the men led Grandmama into the house, the other kept smoking and looking at the garden. It was all right; he couldn't have known I was there, watching him. Sometimes I thought about how there were people who didn't know I existed at all. It was getting dark. For a long time nobody came out. I tried to imagine the house search. The attic. The cellar. Sometimes, when Grandmama left the house, I'd rummage around in the closets. I was afraid that in the cellar they'd discover our other apartment, the one we built in the winter. One of the men came out, carrying suitcases that scraped along the gravel path. They'll probably move away from here. And now the other man was there, too. Together they went back into the house. Or maybe their father had come back from Argentina. The men carried a table out to the terrace. Grandmama still hadn't come out. They went back in again. The two of them carried out an armchair. The other chairs they just threw out, one after the other, sliding the chairs along the smooth stone. One of them got stuck on something and tipped over. There were some loud words, then everything went quiet again. All I could think of was that either they were moving away or going on vacation. And yet I knew that's not what it was. The night before I dreamed that Grandpapa was standing in the middle of the room because he had to leave. Still, I believed that if I hugged him, if I cried, if I begged him not to go, he would stay. But as I pressed my face to his I felt how stubbly it was, because he used to shave only every other day. When Grandmama came home she said she was very tired. She'd tired herself out. She put her white hat and white pocketbook on the table. "We found ten kilograms of sugar, two large containers of fat, and thirty pairs of nylon stockings. Thirty. And all that jewelry!" She shut the window so the bugs wouldn't come in and buzz around the light. She promised that if I went to bed with no trouble she'd tell me the legend of Genaéva.

When Grandpapa died, Grandmama filled the largest pot with water and put it on the stove. She poured two handfuls of salt into it and some black powder and then kept stirring. In the boiling brew she cooked her brown, gray, and dark-blue dresses until they were black. It was too bad about the gray one, I really liked that dress, especially when she wore it with the gold butterfly brooch. Only her satin dress with the big flowers she didn't cook, she left it the way it was—black flowers on a white background. At home, in bed, she'd wear the black dress that had been brown, but when she left the house she'd put on a different black dress, the gray one. The gold butterfly she kept in a steel box and she always carried the key with her. From the window of my room I could see the garden gate. The windows were very high, the sills very wide, because the house was very old. If Grandmama left the house I'd run to the window to peek after her, to see her disappear among the trees in the street. Sometimes she'd come back because she forgot something. She was afraid something might catch on fire, and while she was standing in line at the market I'd go up in flames. I thought about that, what that would be like. My head could just get through between the two middle uprights of the iron bars. I would open the window and slip out. Or, if the house caught on fire in the summer, the window would be open anyway. Gábor said his father told him that if someone's head can get through an opening there is nothing to be afraid of, because that means his whole body can get through. But Gábor probably made that up, because his father is in Argentina, which is where he sends those packages from. They got chocolate and figs, too, in the packages. I had to stand by the window for a long time. Grandmama sometimes would be halfway to the store and then turn back to check the pilot light in the bathroom. The pilot light might set the house on fire. We did have a couple of boxes of matches in their cellar, but it was Gábor and Éva who got them. When Grandmama left she locked the door to the house, and the garden gate, too. She said not to let anybody in, no matter who might come. "Only your father!" But nobody ever came. I imagined how I would set the house on fire. If I had two flint stones I could rub them together until a spark would fly out and ignite the dry moss. That's how Grandpapa made fire when he was left alone in the woods. But I didn't know which stone was a flint stone. In the movies I saw how fire spread. First the curtains, then the floor, the furniture. All aflame. Then the fire leaped from the windows to the roof. The tiles were crackling. On the chimney a German cat. And then the castle got another direct hit and the German cat burned up. There were no people on the street. If I made a move, the floor creaked. I liked that because I knew it was a sound only I could hear. I imagined Grandmama walking on the street. Had to be careful not to imagine her too fast. I'd rather imagine her twice, to let a good long time go by. The house in ruins was a lot like the castle in the movies. At the top of the steep street. At the spot from which we took off with our sleds. When she reached the ruined house I knew I was really alone. If I didn't make the floor creak, it was like somebody else being in the room with me. But no matter which way I looked, he would be watching me from behind my back. Maybe he wasn't even watching from my room but could see through the wall. I looked under the bed, too. And if I opened the door somebody could hide behind it. That's why I had to look behind the doors, too. Grandmama said that her grandmother had told her stories about the white wall serpent. This serpent lives in the wall. At night, in the great silence, it can be heard crawling inside the wall, eating away at it. If it crawls out of the wall, it means somebody is going to die in that room. Every house has its wall serpent. It's not green or brown, and it's not speckled, but completely white, like the wall. It never moved during the day, only the floor creaked if I walked on it. In the hallway a huge mirror hung over the telephone, and in this mirror I could see myself talking to myself on the telephone. A dark room opened from the hallway; it was full of closets and had no windows. And it, too, had a large mirror hanging on the wall. I could look at myself in it when I put on different clothes. The green velvet dress I wanted to give to Éva so she could wear it when we went to the party. Around the waist of this dress, inside a small pouch sewn into the lining, I felt some hard little thingamajigs. When I cut open the pouch with scissors, small gray disks fell out. I showed them to Gábor and Éva and told them that these were gold pieces left for us by our ancestors, who had painted them gray so other people wouldn't know what they were. Gábor took one and tapped it against his teeth. He said they weren't made of gold but of lead and they could be melted down. Before melting them down he asked me to come with him somewhere, but told Éva to stay because where we were going was none of her business. Éva didn't want to stay in the room. Gábor and I went into a room I'd never been in before. Éva ran out into the garden, crying, because Gábor beat her up. A piano stood in the middle of this room, its lid propped up with a rod. I went to the piano and looked inside because I thought that was the reason we'd come to this room. Grandmama told me that once she had a child who died because somebody was careless in propping up the lid of the grain bin and the lid fell on the child's head. I really liked the inside of the piano, because all the wires were nice and straight. But it wasn't the piano he wanted to show me, only a bottle he took out of the closet, full of some white stuff. He wanted me to smell it. It was pretty stinky. "You don't know what this is, do you?" He was shaking it in front of my nose. "That's where they squirt the cream so Mother won't get pregnant!" At the bottom of the closet I found a large paper box. We could rummage around in it for a long time because they kept lots of things in it. Shawls made of silk. A velvet handbag studded with beads and with nice soft leather inside. Two fans. Brown photographs. Letters in pink-lined envelopes. In the photographs, people I didn't know. A woman sitting on a camel and behind her you could see two pyramids. In another picture this same woman leaning against a railing and looking at the water, seeming very sad. There was a picture in which she was in a big hat and laughing. This big hat, folded up, was also there in the box, but in the picture the hat was prettier and the woman's belly was large. I found a brassiere stuffed with foam-rubber breasts. I kept squeezing them. I could tear out little pieces of rubber, but they weren't good as erasers. I also found some kind of instrument in the box; hard, black, long; at one end it had a hole; at the other end of this long black part was a red rubber ball. I could take this ball off the black thing. If I filled it with water, screwed it back on the black thing, and then squeezed it, the water squirted out through the hole. Sometimes I'd stand up on a chair and pee into the sink. In the bathroom I found a secret door. In the closet, behind the robes, was a big white button. At first I didn't know what it was for. But I kept pushing and turning it until I found out. I'd go into the closet and pull the door shut behind me. It would get dark and warm. In that strange smell of dressing gowns, I'd feel out where the button was. If I yanked it hard enough a little door would open in the rear wall of the closet and I could crawl out under the stairs. I knew that if ever I was chased by somebody I could escape through this secret door. One time I opened this door, but I didn't get to the place under the stairs. Everybody was already gone. On the wall they left a long mirror in a gilt frame. Dark curtains covered the windows. But you couldn't see out. Once when the people were still here, somebody said that the curtains were not to be drawn open. But the door was ajar and I could walk into the other room. I started walking and I could see myself in the mirror, walking. I was looking at myself because I didn't think it was me but somebody who looked like me, walking in my place. But it *was* me. I recognized the shoes on my feet, gold shoes with high heels which I'd forgotten to put back in their box. And I could see the line of rooms, one empty room after the other, and everywhere the dark curtains. The candles in the chandeliers were not lit but it wasn't dark. Light was coming from someplace. I wasn't frightened, Grandmama couldn't see me here, but it wasn't very good, because I could only go forward, and from every room another one opened, just like the one before, and from there another, and I didn't know how long I'd have to keep going before I'd get there. I'd been sent somewhere. Maybe if I could peek out into the garden I could figure it out! The curtains were moving a little. Behind them there were no windows! Why? But I did remember where the different pieces of furniture used to stand; after all, I used to live here, and now I'd simply been sent back here. In the meantime, everything had changed. All dusty. Needed a good cleaning. I didn't see a broom anywhere. Then it occurred to me that in the last room everything had stayed the way it used to be, in the very last room, and I started to run through the rooms and the mirror ran with me, I could see myself running. And in the last room everything really had stayed the same. And the bed was there. As if people had only just got out of it: the big quilts folded to the side, and the wrinkles on the pillows and the sheet were pressing against my body. A nightgown was draped on the armchair under which the chamber pot was full of pee. Lying in bed I could see through the open doors the line of rooms, one empty room opening into the next. On the night table was this candlestick and a book and a glass of water. On the surface of the water a thick layer of dust was sleeping. Quickly I looked out the window. It was raining. I touched the pillow, but it was hard. Behind the armchair the secret door was half open. Quickly I opened it. I was standing in a cellar, and above me the chair was still making a racket. Pipes were running here from all directions. Long, winding pipes. They led into the well, but the well was so dark and deep I couldn't see the bottom of it, no matter how far I leaned over. It was dark under the stairs, too, but not as dark as in the closet. This is where we'd pushed an old armchair, the one whose leg broke when Uncle Frigyes sat in it. Maybe on a steel ladder I could have gone down to the bottom of the well. They were talking about something but didn't tell me what. Only Grandpapa's voice could be heard: "Frigyes!" I kept listening but couldn't make out anything else. "Frigyes!" And suitcases with colored labels stuck all over them. If I hit the suitcases with the palm of my hand they sounded like drums, each with its own special sound. This is where the broom stood, and the dustpan, and the carpet beater made of woven bamboo. "You want me to beat you with it?" One label showed palm trees under a blue sky. And on another you could see only the blue sky and the blue sea. A white bird flying. "The sea was completely blue because there wasn't a cloud in the sky, and we could sail smoothly." When I was the child, Gábor liked to tell about the storm, too. "Sometimes we'd see a whale. They'd rise out of the water and blow. Hungry whales go wild, have a whale of an appetite. They were all around the ship, because whales, if they want to, can swim faster than a ship. People thought they could just stand there and watch them. This was a very big ship. It had a movie house, a theater, and a tennis court. It had about a hundred sails and a hundred jibs. Suddenly, as the people were standing there by the railing, a whale blows up a huge jet of water, throws itself up in the air, and bites off a woman's head. Cracking it really loud with its huge teeth. And the woman kept standing by the railing as if nothing had happened, except she didn't have a head. Well, everybody ran below deck, inside the ship. Only I stayed on deck. I climbed up the mast and gave the signal. Nobody noticed me doing it, luckily. But our ship did appear in the distance. It was coming really fast. The captain was afraid to come on deck because of the whales, he was only looking out through a little porthole. The pirate ship is coming! Pirates! What should he do? Black flag on the pirate ship. I kept signaling with a white handkerchief. The sky was beginning to darken. By the time the pirate ship was really close, it was thundering. And lightning. Frogs were falling from the sky. The captain had never seen anything like it before. Waves shot across the deck and whales were flying on top of the waves. I gave the last signal. The captain ran out on deck and wanted to shoot me, but in that instant a huge wave came, and splash! I threw him into the sea. Then the pirates steered alongside us and jumped over. They hugged me and kissed me. We robbed the big ship. Took everything we wanted." With a knife I scraped the valuable labels off the suitcases. The ones with the palm trees and the blue sea I gave to Csider, because he gave me cartridges in exchange. Cartridges he stole from his father. The stairs led to the upper floor. That's where they lived while Grandpapa could still walk. Grandpapa would come down the stairs slowly, holding on to the railing. But he didn't want to live downstairs because his armchair was upstairs in front of the window, and from there he had such a nice view of the garden. After lunch Grandpapa would fall asleep in his armchair. When he couldn't walk anymore, they put his armchair in front of the window in the other room, and there, too, he'd fall asleep in the afternoon, just as he had upstairs. With his mouth open he would breathe so loud it was as if he had something in his throat. Just before he'd fall asleep, Grandmama would wake him. "Papa, don't go to sleep!" Grandpapa would try to open his eyes, but he'd fall asleep again. "Papa, take your teeth out!" Grandpapa would reach into his mouth and put his teeth on the windowsill. Sometimes they'd fall behind the radiator. Then they'd call me to look for them because they couldn't bend down. Once, the denture broke. While it was being fixed, Grandpapa had no teeth. I was scared to reach in under the radiator because I couldn't see what might be in there. My hand touched a soft pile of dustballs. Grandpapa was laughing. "This is only half of it! Find me the other half! Look, Mama, my denture broke in half!" While he didn't have his teeth he talked as if he were chewing something at the same time. "Everybody has to live the life he was given. The impatient ones are unhappy. Remember that! But what is happiness? Who knows? Happiness, I tell you, is best compared to the most beautiful of women. If you want her, if you are doing everything to get her, she may flirt, wiggle her behind, but she won't give herself to you. That's how it is. If you want her soul, she'll give you her body; if you hanker for her body, she'll spread her soul at your feet. Always the part you don't want. That's right. Impatient people are unhappy because they always want something and always get what they don't want. That's why happiness is like the most beautiful woman. It's a mystery. It takes brains, brains! If you pretend not to notice her, if you pretend not to give her a thought, she'll throw herself at you, panting. Finesse, that's what you need to manage in life, finesse. Cunning. You've got to know how to outfox, cheat, and fool even yourself, if you have to. That's how I've done it! Acting as if I didn't wish for anything or want anything! Letting the years go by while I sit around, huddle and crouch, biding my time, waiting for the right moment. Yes, that's how I've done it! And what's happened? What have I gained? I've always been laughed at. Well, let them laugh. The unhappy ones! The idiots! They just don't know! They don't know that one must not seek happiness outside, only inside. You understand? Inside. In yourself! You must feel happiness in yourself, and when you do, never let it go! You mustn't! Not for an instant! If you let it go for the wink of an eye, that miserable happiness of yours will fly off and its place will fill with spit and snot. And then you'll be full of desires, waiting impatiently for other pleasures you may get, and there's no end to it, because all your pleasures will fill you with the lack of some other pleasure. Then something will always be missing. Missing! Missing! Then you'll want more and more, you'll want to gobble and to gorge yourself, because something is missing! then all you'll want is to be filled up, you bottomless pit of a belly, you endless guts and gizzards, you rectum! because something is missing! always missing! Then you will suffer. Then you will endure the filthiest sufferings, insatiable animal that you are, loving to stuff and ram and shove everything into yourself until you're choking on your own vomit. A beast! Not human! A beast! Yet this suffering is not you. What you are is living happiness itself, who receives when he wants not, and has pleasure though he asks not for it. Manna from heaven. Take care! If you want it to, it won't come. Be on the lookout. Be cunning. Bide your time. Don't suffer! You understand? You are not suffering! Understand? You are happy, satisfied, born to be happy. Understand? If you suffer, it's not you but the slimy, snotty beast inside you that suffers. Chase him away, see how he flees! You are happy. Let them all laugh, unhappy idiots. No matter how loud they laugh, you must listen only to the sound of your happiness. Within you. Inward. In here! But even that doesn't mean the fight is over, because you've got those impulses, those drives. Back in my day the whorehouses were in Magyar Street! I tell you, I was a twenty-four-year-old man and a virgin. Go ahead, all of you, go ahead and laugh! Unhappy ones! I was twenty-four, a man, and a virgin. And full of healthy desires. But those youthful instincts! Forbidden!

Mustn't give in! They were forbidden, and I didn't let them fool my desires. Still, at night, in bed, I was lost no matter how hard I tried to hold out whenever a naked woman crossed my dreams. Yet I never touched a woman and I never tapped my own body for pleasure, either, because I was preserving myself for the moment I knew would have to come. I waited! How reluctant Noah was to lose his virginity, no matter how much they egged him on. He waited. He waited until God found Naamah for him, Enoch's daughter, the only woman since Istehar who'd remained pure in that depraved generation. I waited!" If Grandmama came into the room she would make some noise by pushing the chairs around so that Grandpapa would notice, and if he didn't, then Grandmama would also start shouting. "Again? You're doing it again? Papa, don't you realize you're talking out loud?" "Out loud? What do you mean loud?" Grandpapa would yell. "In front of the child! Telling him things like that!" But the louder she wanted to shout the softer her voice became and the louder Grandpapa's. "In front of the child? The child already knows everything! Life is already in the child, just as a single drop has all the ocean in it!" "Oh, shut up, you and your ocean!"—Grandmama was whispering, even though she wanted to yell, but she started to cough—"Ocean!" Whenever Grandpapa was not allowed to talk, he would press both his hands between his knees and fall asleep. His teeth on the windowsill or on the table. I liked to sit nearby and watch him sleep. His mouth would open, he'd breathe loudly, as if the whole room were breathing along with him. I noticed that if I sat opposite him and listened to his breathing long enough, my own breath would also go in and out slowly and exactly at the same time as Grandpapa's. Try as I might to do it differently, his breathing seemed to be controlling mine. Then I'd grow sleepy. I also noticed that if I kept watching him for a very long time without falling asleep, he'd close his mouth, smack his lips, and look at me. I liked it when he looked at me. One afternoon, while I was lying on the bed, it was very dark but I didn't know whether I was awake or asleep, I kept feeling around to find out where I was. But touching things around me didn't help, it was so dark I had no idea where I was. I was groping about for a long time and still I couldn't see anything, only blackness, the kind of blackness in which you can't see anything, and I had no clue how I'd gotten to where I was, or where I was, or whether I was asleep, because everything around me was very hot, and it seemed to me as if in this blackness some other blackness was groping, trying to catch me, and I knew I was reaching out, too, and I thought my hands felt something but I couldn't tell exactly what, and somebody, I don't know why, kept screaming, a terrible scream, but I didn't know who, because I didn't know where I was, only when it became light, when somebody turned on the light, did I realize that I was in my room, sitting on my bed, and everything was in its place, only I was screaming, without knowing why, and it was getting dark outside. That's the kind of look Grandpapa would give me. And when he did that he wouldn't shout, only raise his finger and say something. And then he'd ask me to give him his teeth. I'd bring them over to him, then go back to my place. He would raise his finger again. "Listen! Listen well! I have to tell you I was wrong. Made a mistake. If they hadn't smashed in the door with an ax, if I could have succeeded then, I wouldn't have had to wake up now. All my life I've been waiting for that moment, which may be coming now. I'm still here, aren't I? I was sitting in my own blood in a bathtub, and they smashed in the door. I was only twenty then, and I didn't know this. You wouldn't have a father, and you wouldn't be here, either. Or maybe you would, but not the person you're going to become. Because my blood, the blood that didn't spill into that tub, flowed into the two of you. *Das ganze ist ein Dreck!*"*

* "It's all crap."

When Grandmama died I took out the largest pot. I filled it up with water, but then I couldn't lift it. I couldn't find the black powder. In the kitchen cabinet, behind the flour and sugar, there was a sausage wrapped in paper. When Grandmama came back from the market, she would always hide the sausage in different places so I wouldn't eat it. And I found some candles, too. We made potato paprikash with sausage. She'd cut the onion into small cubes and fry it in fat. I did the stirring. When Grandpapa was alive we didn't cook with fat, only with oil, because his stomach couldn't take it. Grandmama said that even store-bought fat was better than oil because fat was nourishing. The house she was born in stood opposite the church. They'd slaughter as many as four hogs in one winter and always had plenty of lard. With Grandmama we went to visit relatives. They put lots of meat and sausages on the table. The sun was shining in the courtyard, and they said I shouldn't do anything while they went to church. I kept throwing pebbles into the well, and still they weren't back. By the time they returned I was in the pantry eating sausages. I had to climb on top of a sack to reach them. They killed a chicken, but it ran away, its head dangling to the side. I put the sausage on a plate, next to it I put bread and a big knife. First I cut a little piece of sausage and quickly ate it. Then I cut a thicker slice and didn't eat it so fast. In the relatives' house Grandmama and I slept in the same bed. I threw up in the middle of the night and they changed the linen. When I wanted to cut another thin slice, the knife slipped into my finger. I could see inside my finger. But then the blood came out and started to flow, it flowed across my hand and dripped onto the plate, and still it kept flowing. I got up to go to the bathroom, and I felt I was about to fall down. But I didn't, only I couldn't feel my feet and hands, and my head felt much bigger and my finger didn't hurt; everything felt good, because the door opened and the tile floor slammed into me, the black-and-white squares, and they turned gray and I felt I was snuggled into something very white in this I-don't-know-where softness. It was nice and cold. Black and white. I was waiting for Grandmama to come. When I slid down on the railing from upstairs, Grandmama put a cold compress on my head because it swelled up. "God in heaven, what more do I have to endure with you? You do something like this again and I'll put you in an institution! I swear I will! Lucky that you didn't crack your head wide open!" In the institution the stone floor was the same as the one when they took me to the hospital. I remembered that I'd fainted. And all my blood was going to flow out of me. I saw my own hand on the stone floor. Nobody came. Sometimes I imagined how nice it must be for a house like this to have so few people in it. But the house best off is the one that nobody lives in. I stood in the middle of the room and didn't move so I wouldn't disturb the house. If I stood like that long enough the house started to stir. Especially the wooden stairs. And there was noise from upstairs, too. But if I was upstairs then I heard noises downstairs. If I went upstairs, one stair would warn the next. Once I told Grandpapa about this. Grandpapa commended me. "The observation is very correct and precise. Observation is the basis of all knowledge, but we must try to organize our observations into some system. In my youth I read a lot of Hegel, it's a family tradition with us. My grandfather, your great-great-grandfather, had books brought to him directly from Berlin and Vienna, even though he was only an innkeeper. Everything that's in this world is alive. The world itself may be imagined as the largest living animal, because even a house, like everything else, is born, it lives and then dies, and that's all life is. This thought, of course, is more characteristic of the pantheists, like Bruno and Spinoza. But ultimately the idea is not alien to Hegel either, only his world is permeated not by the soul but by reason, the intellect." "Why are you filling his head with such nonsense again?" "That's why you must go on observing relentlessly, but don't get lost in details; systematize. However, don't ever think that your system is perfect, because above all systems stands God the Almighty." After they no longer lived upstairs, Grandmama thought I spent the afternoons in the garden, but I went up to the attic. The attic door was made of steel and creaked. This is where the ancestors lived whom Grandpapa had talked about. Once Csider came up here, too. We stepped carefully so they wouldn't hear us downstairs. If we climbed on the rafters, he could somehow pull up and move aside a roof tile and we could look out and see the garden. I couldn't pull up the tile by myself; Csider figured it out. He said that we should look in the crates. The crates were nailed shut. He said that if his father was a spy and was in touch with my father, and if they kept their secret documents in these crates, then we would expose them. My dog was sniffing the grass among the trees. He wasn't yet dead at that time. But we didn't find the documents. The candlestick was there, the one that almost fell on Grandpapa's head when he was walking on the street. I recognized it because Grandpapa had told me how it banged onto the sidewalk in front of him and when he picked it up he saw it had been dented pretty badly, and when he looked up he saw a man leaning out the fifth-floor window. The man shouted to beg Grandpapa's pardon and asked him to come upstairs if he wouldn't mind. Grandpapa did go upstairs, taking the candlestick with him, and then he asked to keep it as a souvenir. The one who leaned out the window was Frigyes, I called him Uncle Frigyes, and God not only saved Grandpapa's life but also presented him with a good friend. Uncle Frigyes told him that he had recently married, but that his wife always made him so angry he could hardly contain himself. Even when they were engaged they had lots of fights, but they thought things would improve after the wedding. He wanted to throw the candlestick at his wife, that's how angry he was at that moment, but luckily the candlestick flew out the window and luckily it hadn't killed Grandpapa. His wife had locked herself in the bedroom and was weeping. But he hoped that soon she'd get over it and, as the lady of the house, would invite Grandpapa for lunch. If Grandpapa had no other plans. Uncle Frigyes then went to console his wife, who soon came out of the bedroom, laughed, and made light of the whole thing. After lunch they popped open a champagne bottle to celebrate, because all three of them had survived. There was also a broken-down sofa in the attic, that's where we sat. I wanted to tell the story about the storm, but Csider said it was all very stupid and we should be doing something else. He had a bigger one. I thought I heard somebody coming up the stairs. Csider leaned forward, stuck out his tongue as if about to throw up. But nobody came. He got up and left, but I stayed. I thought he only hid somewhere under the rafters and wanted to scare me, but he must have left, quietly. I was afraid he might run into Grandmama. But Grandmama didn't say anything. It rained for a long time and the room where Grandmama listened to the radio started to leak. Grandmama went up to the attic. She got very frightened. Somebody had been up there and moved some of the tiles. Grandpapa thought of the chimney sweep. After I lay on the stone floor for a long time I started to cry, really loudly, so Grandmama would hear. But then I remembered that she was dead. I got up because the floor was cold. The sausage was there. I rewrapped it and put it back into the kitchen cabinet. Candles were lit at Grandpapa's funeral. But I didn't know what to do with the blood. I took out a candle. When we went with our relatives to the cemetery where Grandmama's parents were buried, we'd lit candles then, too. It was getting dark. They let me go up to the attic with the chimney sweep. He opened a little door in the wall which I hadn't noticed before. "Well, kid, we'll beat the daylights out of these ghosts!" He took a chain with a big steel ball at the end and stuck it into the chimney. I could hear the steel ball drop down inside the wall. "Only I'm allowed to open these small doors, you know? This is where they live, in this hole. You can see how dark it is, can't you? I go from house to house and kill them all. I keep yanking on this steel ball. Like this. And then slap them over the head, really hard. You'll see! When they die, nothing's left of these bad ghosts except dirt, black soot." I didn't dare tell Grandmama that it was Csider who had pulled up the tiles, because I was afraid. "A third attack will finish you off! No, Papa, I don't want to get it through my head that you're going to be gone!" "No mortal should interfere with God's affairs!" "Still, if it turns out that He takes me to Himself first, please dress me in my black velvet dress, and don't forget to put my underwear on me, too! And shoes! I keep thinking how we didn't put shoes on poor Lidi!" I always heard them talking after they turned off the lights. Before the gray disks I'd found in the green velvet dress were melted down we played with them, rolling them around the floor. And I asked Gábor about ghosts. The chimney sweep had been to their house, too, but ghosts are white, Gábor said, not black. Éva came in from the garden and said that if we let her play with the disks she wouldn't tell her mother that we'd taken a look at the cream bottle in the bedroom. She had spied on us and seen it. In the evenings their mother always left the house because she had her shows to do. Once they asked me to come over after bedtime. I waited until Grandpapa and Grandmama went to sleep. I had to climb out the window because Grandmama took the key out of the lock. At home their mother didn't sing, only played the piano. In the evening a fellow came for her in a car. "Always some foreign car in front of their house!" Grandmama said. Standing at the window I too could see the car, its red lights were pretty in the dark. With Grandmama we went into town to buy new sandals. I outgrew the old ones. "Go in a cab! Take a cab!" Grandpapa shouted. Grandmama didn't want to. Grandpapa ordered the cab over the telephone. It was very hot. In the cab I kicked off my sandals so they wouldn't hurt. But as soon as we turned the corner Grandmama made the cabbie stop; I had to look for my sandals under the seat, and the cabbie was yelling furiously, "What the fuck are you jerking me around for?" We had to get out. Grandmama gave the man some money, but he went on yelling, "Old slut!" We took the bus into town. I was forbidden to talk about this. Grandmama got into a fight with the bus conductor, who said I had to have a ticket, too. I would have liked to have one. He asked me if I was going to school, but I couldn't answer because Grandmama was yelling. Then the conductor grabbed me and shoved me against some rod and said I was exactly one meter twenty centimeters, anybody could see that. "But he doesn't go to school, he is not six yet!" "At this rate, madam, he'll never go to school, either, such a little idiot!" I thought they could see on me what we had been doing in the attic. I looked down to check my fly, maybe I'd left it open. Everybody was yelling and nodding that the conductor was right. Still, we didn't buy me a ticket. A boy carrying a violin in its case pretended not to see any of this. He was looking out the window. Grandpapa said artists didn't care about the world. I looked out the window, too. Grandpapa liked to tell stories about life. "The two absolutes in seeking God! Every absolute is a lie! Don't run after absolutes if you want to live. Other crazies will do that for you. Monks and artists, eternal seekers to whom we tip the flag of our respect, even though they are lying charlatans. The artist shuts himself up in his room, draws all the curtains, and scrutinizes himself in his mirror. But what can such a lousy mirror really show? The body. Of course the body. He exclaims happily, he who is so unhappy yells happily, God is in the body! Every body is a separate God! Man is God! He's lying! The monk makes his cell so narrow that he can't get into it, and in front of the door he has to take off his self and leave it outside along with his coarse robe. And in place of the neglected and humiliated little body it is the boundless soul that's groping in space, and when this nothing finds its nothing, the mouth exclaims, It's there, it's above me! He's lying! Above me! He's lying! So where is God, if not in the body and not in the soul? Does He exist at all?" "Grandmama says He does." "Oh, come on! Grandmama! Surely she must know? Ask her, has she ever talked to Him? Once, after a very long spiritual dry spell a saint asked God, Where have you been until now, O Lord? and God answered, *Within you!* Oh yes, but if you're looking for Him within, then He's outside, and if you're looking for Him outside, then He's within. *Dazwischen*, always *dazwischen*! Remember that well! Not body and not spirit, yet body as well as spirit. God's countenance is to be sought in innocence, not in pride and not in humility. While you guard your own innocence. If you yield to the body, it will take over, spread over your life like a cancer, you'll drown in your pride. If you yield to the spirit, it will take over, spread over your life like a cancer, you'll drown in your humility. I am free. I say, Long live the body! But I am also a thinker, and I say, Long live the spirit! Old as I am, when my body and my soul have had their day. I am a freethinker! I deny Him, curse Him, besmirch Him with my obscenities. I am not a believer. Still, He is always here because I think. Everything, everything disappears, save this word. And the word exists, therefore He exists, too, He who is designated by the word. If I could finally end this continuous thinking, the word would disappear and He would cease to exist, too. But where would He disappear to? And where would I be myself? Where would I be without my thoughts? Whither shall I go from thy spirit? or whither shall I flee from thy presence? If I ascend up into heaven, thou art there: if I make my bed in hell, behold, thou art there. Should I tell you the story of the suit? When arriving at the real questions, when it should really make an effort, the mind, incapable of thinking, tries to soothe itself with little anecdotes, you see? Well, I'll tell you the story anyway. But I warn you, don't look for edification here. Stories are nonrecurring details of life that offer no lessons to be learned. You can only find *inzwischen*, always between two stories, between two breaths: *dazwischen*!" I was scared because Grandpapa was yelling very loudly. "The story of my suit had to do with our family getting ready to go to the summer resort of Abbazia. Summer. In those days, schoolboys wore short pants with kneesocks. Those days are gone. But shorts with hairy legs like these? And what if we have to visit someone? I'd have been a laughingstock. My legs were good and hairy by that time because God blessed me with powerful natural qualities, may He do the same for you, too. But why shouldn't we be the object of laughter? Clowns are laughed at, too. Don't ever be afraid of being laughed at. If you are among them but not with them, people will laugh at you. Unhappy creatures. But don't be afraid. And don't suffer! You understand? Where was I? When they took me to the tailor and my suit was finished, made of some checked material, the tailor was somewhere in Újvilág Street, I stepped out on the street in my new suit and I was happy. I still remember the trees, a warm breeze was blowing, it was early summer. And I was just luxuriating in the false happiness of outer appearances. Those days are gone. Happiness also melted into thin air, it's gone, no matter how much I talk about it. It's my present happiness I'm trying to smuggle back into that dead picture. As I walk down the street, I can see the street. And all the shiny store windows were reflecting me, me, my image! And all those faces! And the women, whom I was always afraid to look at because I felt it was my mother walking in every woman, and I was full of this filthy something which anybody could see, all they had to do was look at me, I was full of it, you understand? I am full of dead images!" Grandpapa was crying. "Pay attention, but forget everything I'm telling you. Pay attention to what's behind the words, but forget the rest. Don't hold on to images, don't keep them for your old age. Only the thoughts must remain, the pure ideas!" Grandmama told no stories; she started to tell me legends only after Grandpapa's death. "We had a book, the priest was a good friend of my father, because we always had some good wine, ten acres of arable land, two acres of vineyard with good sandy soil, the house I was born in stood opposite the church, and my father was a deeply devout man, our garden ran all the way to the cemetery, it was full of fruit trees, cherry, sour cherry, walnut, plum, and Father gave generously to God's church, in the evening they played cards, often, because the teacher from Zsánli and the pharmacist from Bogdány also came over, we had no apothecary in our village, if the priest's land needed manure it was Father who brought it, or if he was expecting guests it was Father who went to fetch them with the surrey, it was only a buggy but everybody called it a surrey because we had not only a carriage but also this buggy, we used it to deliver milk and cream to the Danube-palace, and Father couldn't even read or write, people used to ask me, Why are you reading so much? yet when I told them about the legends they liked to listen, but Father was a rich and proud man, when he was on his deathbed he had the priest summoned, he confessed and he left this world without a complaint, he said I was the one who caused him the greatest suffering because I and Béla Zöld wanted to be together, but Béla Zöld was Protestant, my father kept yelling, my mother would have liked me to be Béla Zöld's wife, people even said that it wasn't me but my mother who was in love with Béla Zöld, but Father kept yelling that if I married a Protestant he'd burn a cross into my body, I must know forever where I belonged, he'd chase me naked across the village, but that's not what I want to tell you, even though all my problems started with that, but that's not what I want to tell you about, but the book we got from the priest, and it was full of legends, things that really happened, on the cover of it there was this large angel with its wings spread, about to fly up to heaven, and these were the legends I told the people in the village." When she thought I was already asleep, Grandmama would go back to her room but without closing the door. At night, if I woke up, I saw her standing by the window. She said she was sure that if she hadn't fallen asleep that night, Grandpapa wouldn't have died, and now it was her punishment that she couldn't fall asleep, she had to wait for the hour of Grandpapa's death, because every night she had to go and bring Grandpapa back, because sometimes she thought he hadn't died and the whole thing was only a prank. One night I woke up and Grandmama was standing in the middle of my room wearing the green velvet dress from which I had cut out the lead disks, and something was shining in her hair. She was coming toward me, had her arms stretched out, she was very angry and slapped me in the face, and I felt she had something hard in her hand, only I couldn't see what, it was so dark, but the slap didn't hurt. In town we were walking in the street and Grandmama was very beautiful because she was wearing her white hat and the silk dress with the black-on-white pattern. She said that all these houses had been destroyed during the war, all of them, and everybody died. I asked if we had also died, but she said no, because we were alive, weren't we? But where was I then, when I was not yet alive? Grandmama started yelling: "Feri! Feri! There goes your father! He can't hear me! Feri!" We were running. Lots of people were coming in our direction and lots of them were ahead of us. "Feri!" Grandmama was running ahead of me, I was behind her, but I couldn't see where my father was among all the people. People stopped, turned around, looked at us, and we were running among them. "Feri! My dearest little Feri!" I didn't recognize his back because I was looking for a uniform. "Feri!" He didn't have his cap on, either. We just looked at him. "What are you two doing here, Mother?" But he wasn't smiling, he just asked her. "He outgrew his sandals!" I looked at my sandals, which pinched my feet. My father hugged Grandmama, then kissed her, and then hugged and kissed me, too. His face was smooth and he didn't stink. He put his hand on my neck, and Grandmama held on to his arm. His palm felt good on my neck. That's how we were, waiting for a streetcar and two cars to pass. He came even closer. "And you're here, in town! And haven't even called?" "Come on, Mother, let's go to that pastry shop." "My God, why couldn't you phone? Why didn't you come home? Did Papa offend you in any way? Or did I?" The streetcar squeaked and its bell was ringing, because we ran across the street anyway, without waiting for it to pass. "Why didn't you come home, if you're here already? Feri!" In the pastry shop I got ice cream in a glass. Grandmama also asked for ice cream but didn't touch it, she was crying. And Father was angry. "Please, Mother, don't make a scene, I beg you. You know very well." "Yes, I do. I know everything. Everything, I know everything." "Please, Mother, stop it, you know what the situation is now. I can never be sure. You know. You know that's the kind of job I have. I can't talk about it. Be glad we've met, and I'd like to be glad about it, too." "I should be glad." "Please wipe your eyes. I've got no time, I've got to go somewhere, I'm in a hurry. It's trouble enough that we've met." "Trouble? Even meeting you like this is trouble?" "Yes, because instead of being glad to see me, you sit there crying. Mother, why not make good use of the little time we have, tell me the news from home. Is Papa all right? You still have some money left? Should I send more? Why don't you answer me? Mother, I haven't time for this sort of thing. Why don't you say something? Believe me, I have trouble enough of my own, and I can't talk to anybody about it. Just try to imagine how hard it must be for me. Please, have a little consideration and say something, Mama, you know I can't bear it when you clam up. Mama!" But Grandmama kept on crying and didn't answer. I pretended to be eating my ice cream and that I was very glad to have ice cream, so that he wouldn't be angry, but he didn't notice that that's what I was doing. Grandmama kept crying, even though she wanted to stop, I could tell, and did want to say something, and she wiped her tears with her hands, but every time she opened her mouth to say something she wound up crying again. He looked at Grandmama and was sad. Then he got up and walked over to a woman whom he paid. He looked more handsome than in his uniform and I would have liked to ask him to take me with him. "Mama, I'm terribly sorry you've ruined this chance meeting, but I must run. As soon as I have some time I'll come home. I don't know when, hugs and kisses to Papa." And he hugged Grandmama, rubbed my head, and left. Lots of people were going in and out of the pastry shop. Grandmama took a kerchief from her white pocketbook and wiped her eyes. Outside, the sun was shining, but in the shop it was quite dark. "God will punish him, too, one day. Just as He's punished me." A woman kept jerking the long arms of the coffee machines, steam was rising.

Lots of people were smoking. Grandmama said, Let's go, but I started crying and said I didn't want any shoes. "I can't get up." Grandmama pressed her hand to her chest. "I can't get up." She tried to get up but couldn't. In the meantime, my ice cream had melted. Again everybody was watching us, and a man next to us asked Grandmama, "Can I be of help, madam? Are you all right?" I tried to help Grandmama, but she couldn't get up. "I'm scared." Everybody was talking in the pastry shop. "I'm scared. I don't know why, I just am. There's nothing wrong, I'm just scared." The man took Grandmama's arm. "Do you feel ill, madam? A glass of cold water, maybe a glass of cold water?" He told the waiter to bring a glass of water and make it really cold. At night, whenever Grandmama would start to breathe hard, the way Grandpapa used to, I immediately took her some water. The waiter was bringing the water and also shouting, asking the honored guests if there was a doctor among them, because in the meantime Grandmama started to slide off her chair. "I'm a nurse!" The woman who said that got hold of Grandmama and splashed some of the water on her forehead, and everybody was standing around us. Grandmama's mouth was open. Grandmama had tied up Grandpapa's jaw with a kerchief. The nurse kept shouting that people should back off because Grandmama needed more air. "In this terrible heat!" Everybody had something to say. "They were fighting with a man just before." I thought of running out of the shop. I stuck my head among the bodies around us, but somebody caught me by the neck. "Where are you going?" They put a chair out on the sidewalk for Grandmama to sit in; people were hanging in bunches on the platforms of the passing streetcars. The nurse told Grandmama to take deep breaths. People stopped and looked at us strangely. I was to tell Grandpapa that we couldn't get sandals in the right size. When the two of them fell asleep I got up. The floor creaked a lot. In front of the window I waited until it was completely quiet. In the other room Grandpapa was breathing very loudly. "Don't snore, Papa! Do you hear me? Stop snoring! I can't fall asleep! Papa!" At night, Grandpapa kept his teeth in water. Grandmama always waited until I fell asleep and then she brought in the chamber pot and a mug with water in it. But I wasn't asleep, I jumped up and kept jumping on the bed and shouting, "She's bringing the potty! Bringing the potty!" Once she threw the mugful of water on me. "Why are you torturing me? Tell me why. Don't I do everything for you? I'm going to tell your father to put you in an institution, I can't take this any more. Lie down this instant, you hear me?" I really could get through between the bars of the window guard. Gábor was lying on the rug because he had had some wine and he was drunk. Éva was dancing by herself in the middle of the room in her mother's dress. We threw pillows at one another. The door opened and their mother walked across the room, naked. In the other room she turned on the radio and put on her robe. She looked at herself in the mirror while listening to the radio. She said she was sure that now they would hang them all because the whole thing was nothing but a big sham. When Éva and I stopped dancing I felt a sharp pain in my side. Gábor couldn't get up. He grabbed a chair, pulled himself up, but slid back down, and his head was nodding all the time. Éva was laughing. Gábor threw up on the carpet. Éva quickly took off her mother's dress and ran out of the room. She had no panties on. When their mother left they'd close the windows and curtains and turn on the chandeliers. Éva would put on some dress. Gábor would put on a record and turn up the volume all the way. He'd take the sword off the wall and start fencing. Once he slashed one of the overstuffed chairs, ripping the velvet. Éva came up with the idea of hanging my dog. Gábor went to look for a rope. We started calling the dog. Clothes were drying on the rope in the garden. He cut it down with the sword. He stood on a chair and tied the rope to the chandelier. We called and called, but the dog wouldn't come. I had to clean up the vomit from the carpet. I could see everything he ate. They said they'd hang me instead. When the lawn was cut we had to rake the grass into a stack. We climbed to the top of the stack. Gábor played Eugénie Cotton, I was Pak Den Aj. We wrestled and I let him beat me because Eugénie Cotton was president of the International Women's League, and Pak Den Aj only president of the Korean Women's Coalition. We turned somersaults. Éva squealed and made a grab at the rope. The chandelier fell out of the ceiling. I didn't dare go home. Among the bushes I waited for something to happen. Csider called me over to their house to try the new swing his father had just set up. He showed me that standing up on it he could go really high. But he flew out of the swing, crashed through the window into the room. His mother came over to see Grandmama and I couldn't convince her that it wasn't me who'd done it. Grandmama was shouting in the garden. I thought maybe she'd found the Nina Potapova textbook which we kept in our apartment in the bushes. But it was my dog she'd found there. Together we took the dog into the house. "Somebody must have poisoned it." Grandmama dug a deep hole. Grandpapa also came out when we buried it.

The next day when I woke up I went out into the garden. The wind was blowing, bending and tearing at the trees. The doghouse was empty. The dog liked to lie under the eaves, in the flower bed. The ground was quite hard at that spot. I called to the dog, telling it to come with me, but it didn't budge. Its head was resting on its two forepaws. It was blinking at me and lazily wagging its tail. I knelt down to stroke it, but above me a window opened, the wind caught it and banged it against the wall, and somebody I couldn't see yelled, "Don't dig up the ground! Don't dig up the ground!" The voice was riding the wind. But the ground should have been dug, it was autumn, the flowers were dried up, and my dog wasn't lying there any more; in his place the ground was hard and a little greasy, and there were a few hairs, small tufts of hair were left there that I should have plowed under, but somebody was still yelling, "Don't dig up the ground!" The wind hurled the voice at me: "Don't dig up the ground!" I wanted to put back the shovel. The window was banging. I started to run, but it was difficult in the deep snow. I ran along the wall of the house, but it was still hard to lift my feet in the thick snow, and it was cold, very cold, and the wind knocked snow into my face. I would have liked to look up to see finally where I was, but I couldn't because the sky was so bright! Down here it was completely dark. If only I could look up at the bright sky! But I had to close my eyes. In the dark. If only I knew what I should do! Then night fell. The next day, when I woke up and went out into the garden, two white butterflies were chasing each other. I ran after them, to see what butterflies do. They were fluttering around each other in glittering circles as they flew, and I ran after them, over the shrubs, over the hedges, out over the wide lawn, if only I had a butterfly net! and then vanished above a bush. Above the bush I couldn't follow them. The sky was blue, clear, and the light blinded me, as if it had sucked up the white glittering of the butterflies. And the silence. The bushes were there, squat and heavy. Hawthorn. Lilac. Elder. Hazel. Not far from the tree where one leaf sometimes stirred, even with no wind blowing. Through the secret passage I crawled under the bushes. In the nursery the bed was nicely made, with hay, good and soft. In the kitchen the pots were up on the shelf. A book lay on the rickety garden chair. I could hear my own panting. The soft haybed was tempting me to lie down and go to sleep, as though I was the child and the two of them had gone to the party, but I couldn't lie down because I kept hearing my own panting as if an animal, some kind of animal, was panting in the bushes, not me, and I could see it. I grabbed the shelf and yanked it out from under the pots, and the pots rattled and clanked, rolling into the bushes, and then for a moment I didn't hear my panting, but then I heard it again. This animal is panting right here, in the bushes! A dog. It was barking. It was scrabbling around, turning everything topsy-turvy. I ripped the haybed apart, lobbed the pots over the fence, and enjoyed hearing each and every thud as they landed; I dragged the garden chair out on the lawn, jumped on it, let the caning rip! let it tear, hang in shreds, the whole chair in smithereens; I tore out the pages of Nina Potapova and tossed its cover into the shrub, where it caught on a branch. I crawled back in, and the dog was barking and panting, its tongue hanging out. The dog was glad that it had finally demolished the house, and now it was sniffing around. But it seemed I smelled the same scent Gábor and Éva had in their hair and skin and also their home. The dog kept sniffing, snuffling in the hay, searching for the smell I thought I had caught for a moment, but the dog lost it. The ground here, under the bushes, was wet and soft. I was watching the dog, wondering what it felt like to nuzzle the ground. The smell of decaying leaves. I took a mouthful of dirt and chewed on it, but I had to spit it out. The dead dog was baring its teeth. I lowered myself, stiffening and stretching out my legs and arms, I felt what the dog must have felt, but it kept on panting, and I tried to hold my breath and not take in any more air, to be motionless, like a corpse. The compressed air inside me started to expand and made me hot, and then it burst. I was breathing slowly. And nobody could have known I was dying there, like my dog. A small leaf was swaying gently back and forth. And on the leaf two tiny very bright eyes. The leaf's eyes were watching! The leaf was rocking up and down at the tip of the little branch. Then I had to breathe because the effort made me so weak, yet I didn't die. Though I would have liked to be dead, if anyone cared to know. Carefully I sucked in a bit of air, and by then things didn't look so reddish and hazy, and then I saw that the leaf didn't really have eyes but that a green tree frog was sitting on it. Green, exactly like the leaf. Its back seemed to be the curve of the leaf itself. I was looking at its eyes and it was looking at mine. As if it weren't alive. But I could also see how its chin was throbbing excitedly, as though its heart were beating right there, under its wide mouth, and it was sitting with its legs spread wide, rocking up and down on the leaf, up and down, ready to jump. When the leaf reached its lowest point I could see the pulsation. Within me the blood was pulsing the same way. But then it seemed as if something awful had happened, some big mistake had been made. I thought I was bigger than a frog, but this frog grew and grew, and I kept shrinking, because it was watching me with its huge eyes, and the more it watched me, the smaller and more insignificant I became. I had to close my eyes, but even then its great strength kept throbbing in its enormous chin, and I had no choice but to wait in the dark for it to pounce on me and gobble me up as it would some insect. When I woke up, the leaf was motionless at the tip of the little branch, just above my forehead. The sun was shining as before. On my open palm ants were crawling, calmly, in orderly file, one behind the other. I locked them into my palm, but they quickly climbed out between my fingers. I thought I had awakened because Grandmama was shouting, calling me in for lunch, but Grandmama was asleep on her bed. I stopped by the door, listening, wanting to know whether she was breathing. The room was dark and cool and full of Grandmama's smell. On the night table a glass of water. On Grandmama's finger the ring with the turquoise stone, the one I will inherit when Grandmama dies. Carefully, so the floor wouldn't creak, I left for the garden. The sun was always shining. I picked up a fallen peach and split it in two. Its juice trickled down my fingers, a white worm was inching its way over the wet pit. I pressed the worm into the meat of the peach. It wiggled, struggled, but I pushed it so far into the soft wet mass that I couldn't see it, and then quickly, worm and all, I popped the peach into my mouth, and careful not to bite down, I swallowed the whole thing. I imagine the worm got to my stomach alive. Now it's down there in the dark, it's alive and has no idea where it is. And still it wasn't evening. Bees arrived. I felt something was wrong with me. Suddenly. It was as if somebody else were sitting in the grass, somebody whose heaviness I could feel, but it wasn't me, and everything was hazy, blurred. Suddenly. A small shred of a cobweb glistened and disappeared in the air. And whatever else I looked at, it wasn't I who was seeing it, that's why everything was disappearing, and I could never tell what it was I'd just seen a moment before, because I could no longer see it. And I'm sure it's like this only with me, and that's why I must be bad. But I must keep this from others and pretend I see everything they see. And I wasn't sitting where I had sat before, but jumped up and hugged the trunk of the peach tree, but still I felt that this wasn't me either, because what I felt was not what I'd felt before; maybe I was this tree trunk, as good and as strong as this trunk. And then I couldn't understand why I was on my knees by the tree, why I was hugging its trunk, and something had to be done so it wouldn't be like that, but I didn't know what. I slid down the tree onto the grass. The grass smelled good, and I opened my eyes very wide, to be rid of this blurry dimness and so I could see the grass. Each blade grew out of the ground, but there was lots of room between them. Empty little paths. If I were a blade of grass, I too would grow out of the ground and stand here among the other blades of grass, I'd be one of them. But some man would come along and knock me down with his hand. I had to jump up and run away. At the gravel path I stopped and looked back. But how could I hide my badness when every little thing was aware of it? Maybe I ought to choose one blade of grass, as if it were my own child, or myself, and then love that blade of grass. I knelt down to choose one. From that position the blades of grass looked like a forest. With enough room for insects to walk among its trees. I blew on the grass, to make a storm, I blew and I shouted and I kept rolling around on the grass, then I threw myself on my back and yelled into the sky, but I had to close my eyes because the sun was very strong. I am lying on blades of grass!

I thought of going into the house and telling Grandmama, but my body started moving on its own and I rolled down the slope; sky, grass, trees, ground, sky, grass, and bushes spinning closer and closer, and all the while I was shouting, I'm lying on blades of grass! lying on blades of grass! and each time I rolled to the ground it shut me up and that felt good. And then the clear sky again, and the shrubs that gave me shade, and the white flowers, too, and I could keep my eyes open and look at things without knowing whether they were close or far away. I should bring a ball to play with. The red ball flew up into the sky. The heavy white calyxes swung gently at the end of the upward-reaching branches. A bee came. It landed on the rim of the cup, strolled around it, then crawled inside, a humming shade on the petals. At dusk the flowers folded up. Down by the fence, as if it were raining huge white drops in the night, falling from somewhere but never reaching the ground. A face among the leaves. But I didn't know whose. Slowly, as if in pain, the man opened his mouth, wanting to say something, but it was very dark inside the mouth and something I couldn't see was moving in that darkness. And all his efforts were in vain. Then he reached out and plucked a flower. He showed it to me, his mouth still open. He wanted me to smell it. I could see inside the flower, but the water inside it flowed out, all at once just spilled out of the flower. "Why did you roll the ball?" and he must not have noticed that the water had come out of the flower because he wasn't at all angry. "Why did you roll the ball?" "I didn't roll it, I threw it, let it fly!" "Why do you say you threw it when you rolled it, I know. I am the doctor. A ball must not be rolled, it has to be thrown for it to fly!" "But I didn't roll it!" "Come on! Throw it?! Can't you hear? The water flowed out! Can't you hear? Come on! Throw it! Up, up!" I looked up to where he was pointing, but another man came through the open door. Click-click, his steps clattered strangely, and of course he noticed I was looking at something and he hurried toward me. "My covers got stained!" "Where?" he asked, and still he kept coming toward me. "Here." Now he was close, very close, took the covers, raised them, and looked. "Where?" "Here." "No, I can't see anything, I can't see, I can't see anything." "But they're stained." "With what?" "With blood!" He opened his mouth, grabbed the covers, pulling them off and stuffing them into his mouth, laughing all the while, and he kept doing it even though his mouth was already full, and I already knew that maybe it wasn't water that had flowed out of the flower but blood, but the way he laughed I had to laugh along with him, at the way he was stuffing the covers into his mouth. And I parted the bush, but didn't find the ball, though I'd seen it roll in there somewhere. And while I was looking for the ball I laughed because I remembered how the man had kept stuffing the covers into his mouth. A bird landed on the branch above my head; it lifted its pointed tail feathers a little and a white limy discharge dribbled down on the leaf where the frog was sitting. Bird shits lime! That too I had to laugh at. The bird turned its head every which way and took off. I wanted to see where it was flying to. I ran among the bushes, leaves and branches knocked against my face, and I could see it flying over to Éva and Gábor's house to have a drink. I heard something crack. An empty snail shell. Thick ivy with dark leaves was growing everywhere under the bushes. In the meantime, the bird flew on, over the house. On the terrace where their mother always yelled for them, a large sunshade, folded around its long pole, had been leant against the railing. Here, the garden seemed even brighter. Here, too, the shrubs were set in a circle around the neatly cut lawn and, in the middle, the calm water of the pool. The tub was floating on the water. I thought that somebody must have stayed in the house after all and was watching me from behind the closed shutters. Maybe I should say that my ball had rolled over here? Every move made a noise. But the shutters did not move, and nobody came out on the terrace, either. I kept listening. Maybe they had a pistol and would shoot me, and all I'd done was to come to look for my ball. It seemed the house was already covered with dust. Still, there must be somebody in there. The barrel of the weapon in the cracks of the shutter. But really, I'm only looking for my ball, honestly, because it was dark when it flew over here and I couldn't find it. Go ahead, look for it! I stepped out of the bushes. If there's nobody in the house, then the whole place belongs to me. I'll move in and everything will be mine. I can sit down at the piano. The sword is mine, too. The rifle above the fireplace and the little picture that glows in the dark—they're mine, too. And the Japanese picture. If they didn't take it with them. And I shall take me a wife and we shall live here. And my wife will wear their mother's dresses, and I shall bring over the green velvet dress I wanted to give to Éva. In the evening a car will come for us, its red light shining bright, and she will put on the green velvet dress to go to the party. The jewels! I know, she showed me, I know where they are! I started to move, pretending to be looking for something in case somebody was watching me from the house, if they had come back, so they could see I was looking for my ball. But I couldn't go on with this game because I couldn't shake the thought that I knew, that they had showed me where the jewels were stashed; and the piano, and the Japanese picture, and the sword, and the rifle. Maybe I should tell them I had left my ball there, in case somebody was in the house after all. What kind of ball? Red, with big white dots. They probably didn't know about the secret passage. And if someone was in the cellar? We didn't see any ball. He probably wanted to steal something. I was shaking and unable to turn toward the house. But I was already in the house, rummaging through the jewels, banging on the piano, poking around, but in the house, behind the window, stood that figure with the weapon, waiting and watching and knowing perfectly well what I'm thinking about. They're not coming back, ever. I felt there was no one there; I had to close my eyes not to see the man with the pistol behind the shutters. There's nobody there. I can go. I could open the heavy steel window of the air-raid shelter. It was hard to open. An iron fastener kept it in place. You had to knock the fastener up with a stone and that made a noise, a short knock making a hollow repeated noise. But nobody would hear it, there was nobody in the cellar, there'd only be me. Enough light came through the open window so that I could see the cellar was empty. I could crawl in through the opening, hold on, and then lower myself into the darkness below. And my feet could already feel the first brick; the bricks put there to make it easier to lower yourself. Once down, I could pull shut the heavy iron window. It creaks. The fastener I could slide back from the inside, too. The bricks wobble under my feet, one more jump and I'm in all the way. Imagination makes the distance greater than it really is, and my knees give a funny little buckle, but I'm already on the pitted surface of the concrete floor. Two shiny lines, like threads, stretch across the darkness; I have to wait for my eyes to adjust so I won't bump into anything. But it's as if I'm dreaming, I am still nowhere. I make the wrong turn and bump into something. That's the crate. You can crawl into the crate and then you're in a house and the cellar is in the house and the crate is in the cellar. Above me is the crate, above the crate the cellar, and above the cellar the house. Above the house the sky. If I crawl into the crate I can imagine all that. I listen to the tiny noises of darkness. It's as if something were crawling about up there, not a person, but not an animal either. I can hear my own breathing. Before I came, the house hadn't heard my breathing, it was resting in its own silence. It's impossible to stay motionless for so long. For only so long can I listen and watch to see if anything moves, or to make sure it's only myself I hear; and if it's just me, and if this breathing, which is my own, becomes more and more relaxed, each breath longer and longer, and if my heart stops pounding and I don't have to press my hand to my stomach to stop the pain, then I can really get started, then I can leave my hiding place, then I can step out from behind the wide frame of the window, and then surely Grandmama won't turn back, and Grandpapa will be sound asleep upstairs. My legs weren't shaking so much any more. No noise was coming from above, and the deep silence down here all around me somehow settled into me. Gábor and Éva could never wait like this; only I can. Which means they're not here. There is nobody up there. Nobody. I propped my hand against the crate, my eyes became accustomed to the dark. The long passage takes a turn under the house. I had to stop and wait after each step, until I didn't hear my footsteps, and then, with my palms on the wall, to prepare my next step. Rough mortar sticking out between the bricks. My feet still hadn't bumped into the bottom of the staircase. Another step on the coarse concrete floor. Another feel of the hands, another step. At last the stairs, and on top of the stairs the door. It's open a crack. Without creaking, the crack widens silently. But the hallway is dark. Warm and musty. Through the crack of the door the hallway smell rolls out, that smell! Though the cold air of the cellar is cooling my back, I am hot, and my inner heat and this outer cold touch my skin at the same time; I shudder. Something rustles among the dark leaves and tangled runners. A dull glitter under two leaves. Smoothly the snake propels itself forward as if swimming on the surface of water. Toward me. And I can't tell where it starts or where it ends, I can only see the glistening of its light brown body under the leaves as it tranquilly propels itself toward me. Then it stiffens into motionlessness. Its gaping mouth and two clever eyes among the leaves. It seems to be staring forward, toward its destination, but in the meantime it sees me as well. Closing its mouth, it too stops breathing. On its steely head darker and thicker scales. Its nose is two holes under the eyes. It could pass for a tendril among the leaves. Stupid little snake. The sun is hitting your head. I couldn't slap or hit it fast enough, it would slip out from under my hand, like a lizard. If I stretched only my arm toward it, not even the shadow would reach it, because the sun shines on both of us from the front, throwing the shadows behind us. I extend my arm very very slowly, so slowly that I can't notice it myself. I must grab it from behind, by the neck. It keeps looking at me, unsuspecting. The body is motionless among the leaves, but its end cannot be seen. I unlock my knees just a hair, to get even closer, and stay that way. As far as I can tell it has made no move at all, must not be thinking about protecting itself. I've got to reach it from behind so it can't bite and squirt the poison into my hand. This last move must be made very quickly, but I don't know how. Now it seems as though it can see what I'm doing, after all; still, it keeps staring ahead, unsuspecting, in the direction it had been moving, toward the pool, yet it appears to be looking at me as well. I am growing weak and tired, but I do want to do it. I can't bend my knees any more or bring my arm any closer. The tiniest rustling sound and I pounce, and I feel its steely head between my fingers, its body is thrashing, my hold on it is clumsy, but its movements are restrained by the leaves, and I am kneeling above it, squeezing and pressing its head into the soft ground, not to let it move before I can get a better grip, and I am shaking and shuddering because it opens its huge mouth, its long tongue like flashing shadows; but I won't let go, and I should be laughing, because my grasp is now firm, but I must squeeze really hard, its mouth is gaping, it can't move its head, only its long body is thrashing behind my arm. It keeps gaping, its long tongue darting quickly in and out. And then I jumped up and raised it in the air. It was as long as my arm. And it was hanging in the air like a stiff rod. But this rod swung to the side and struck my face, a smooth, cold, strong swish across my face; and then it stiffened again, and again it slashed into me, with a bang, a slimy, cool darting across my face, and I no longer felt in touch with the ground, I felt nothing but the snake's neck that might slip out of my hand, from between my fingers, any moment, and that I couldn't go on holding like this and it might free itself, and it stiffened again, but this time it did not strike my face but coiled around my arm, its slippery, cool, thrashing body wrapping itself around my naked arm; I was running toward the pool, somehow to escape, to get free of the snake, I was running but I had no sensation of myself, only of my arm, the coiled body around my arm, this repulsive throbbing and sliding, thrusting and squeezing; and shaking it didn't do any good; what if I threw it into the pool! but how to tear it off my arm? With my other hand? and what if it can breathe in the water? I didn't dare touch it with my other hand; no matter how I shook it, it clung to me, it writhed, I didn't dare tear it off, only kept squeezing its neck, afraid that it would slip out of my grip, and I tightened my hold so that it couldn't move its head at all, but I felt I was growing very tired. And there was a white stone. And I couldn't hold it up in the air anymore. I knelt down and shoved its head into the water, but it was thrashing, it lived, coiled around my arm. With my other hand I picked up the stone. I pulled the snake's head out of the water. It was gasping. On the concrete edge of the pool I began knocking the stone against its head. Every knock felt good, even though I was hitting my hand as well; and I saw it was my hand that was bleeding, but I kept hitting it, hitting it hard, and still it wouldn't get off my arm, and it lived, but I kept hitting it, the stone was all bloody. And I could see there was no head there any more, only some shapeless pulp, a moving lump in the blood, but I kept hitting it because it was still thrashing, wouldn't let go of my arm, but I let go of the stone, it plopped into the water, and I tore the snake off my arm, but still felt it was there, and I was tearing the skin off my arm even though the snake was now thrashing on the ground around its own shattered head. And I couldn't tell whose blood it was, the snake's or mine, on the concrete around the crushed head, and my hand was like the snake's smashed head, as if I were still squeezing and hitting it, but it no longer hurt. I couldn't, I just couldn't get up. The snake was writhing on the dry concrete. I ran. I tripped on something and I couldn't run, but I couldn't fall either; still, I should have been glad it wasn't coiled around my arm any more, but my arm, my fingers kept feeling its body; at last I stumbled and fell down. It felt good to lie on the grass. I was cooling my hand on the grass. It was throbbing. But I couldn't lie on the grass because all the other snakes would be crawling out, coming after me, I had to get up. I felt that the way things were I could never go home again. Silence reigned in the garden except for my own panting. They'd be crawling out from under the bushes. I knew if I looked back it would still be writhing. I'll stay here and nobody will know about it. I let the iron window stay slightly ajar to let in a bit of light. I started walking down the corridor, but it was dark. I groped for the steps. The door was locked. I was sitting in the crate. We had lined the crate with old rugs to make it soft. Outside, the sun was shining, a piece of empty sky. My thigh and my leg cooled my hand. I wondered what would happen if the poison from the snake's mouth had dripped into my bruised hand. I'll die right here in this crate. The blood was becoming gooey, probably because of the poison. I would have loved to fall asleep in the crate, but the poison was stinging my hand. I didn't look, I didn't want to see! I washed my hand at the garden faucet so I wouldn't be bloody if I died, so nobody would know what happened to me. I was sitting in the crate, just staring; outside, the sun was shining. But I had to get out of here, too: even bigger snakes were crawling out of the corner. If the door hadn't been locked I could have taken the sword off the wall and slashed the snake to pieces so it wouldn't wriggle any more. A big green lizard was lying on the ground, on its back, still kicking, but I poured a bunch of pebbles over it and I was frightened, even though it was barely alive. I had to get out of here, too. When I wanted to crawl out of the cellar I saw Csider walking up the terrace steps. I wanted to see what he was doing. He looked in through the glass door. Kicked the pole of the sunshade. It slid along the railing and with a huge bang fell on the stone floor of the terrace. Csider looked around, without moving, listening, to see if anybody was around. He started down the stairs. I quickly pushed out the cellar's iron window and it creaked. "Hey, Csider!" He saw it was only me. In the summer his hair was always close-cropped. He rubbed his head, pretending he wasn't scared. I stayed in the cellar, the bricks wobbling under my feet, but I didn't want him to see my hand. "Can I get in there?" He bent down and looked in. "What's there?" "From here you can go up into the house, but they put a lock on the door from the inside." "Come on, let me crawl in!" Inside, we talked in whispers. The window stayed open. "We have candles and matches, too." Csider walked around the cellar, peered into the corridor, but it was dark there. "They didn't leave any documents behind?" "Probably upstairs. But they locked the door tight shut." Csider checked out everything and climbed into the crate. There was room for the two of us. Éva was always left out. "Listen, Csider, this is something I just made up!" "What?" "Bird shits lime!" He scratched his head. "It's good, eh?" "Their father was a spy," he whispered. "Come on, he went to Argentina a long time ago, that's where he's been sending those packages from." He laughed. "That's where he was a spy!" "I never saw him." "And that woman, the reason she didn't get out of here's because she's a dirty slut." "No!" I said out loud. He went on whispering. "You think we don't know? A foreign car comes around here all the time! You deny that?" "I saw that too, from the window, and Grandmama was the witness!" "She was a dirty slut!" He wanted something, because he climbed out of the crate. I thought that if he knew it, too, then I had to tell him; and I shouldn't have mentioned Grandmama, because that was a secret. "Once we were playing in the room and she came in stark naked. Stark naked." "Don't yell! Stark naked?" "Yes." My hand really hurt and I was afraid he might find the matches and the candle, and I shouldn't have mentioned them, either. "And what's it like?" "Well, completely naked, and it's hairy down there. And she was walking around like that, and we were right there." "Hey, Simon, do you have any paper here?" "Paper? I'm sure there's paper upstairs. But they put a lock on the door. We should open it somehow." Csider came over to me. "Shut up! I told you not to yell!" I couldn't see his face because the sun was shining outside. He was whispering. "I was never friendly with them, not me!" "We should get something to open the door with! They have a picture that glows in the dark. Japanese. And they told me, they showed me where the jewels are! And the sword!" "Sword?" "Come on, Csider, let's do it!" "What?" "What we did in our attic!" "Nah, not now, now I gotta take a shit." He walked into the corner and pulled down his pants. Squatted on his haunches. I kept looking at him. The shit was coming out of him. He squatted there for a long time, and now and then he moaned a little.

One day up in the attic Grandpapa was telling me about our ancestors. Grandmama had brought a fish from the market. She was very glad to have got one because Grandpapa loved fish. She stood in line for two hours, but she couldn't go to church with the fish. When she got wind of something being available at the market she'd take me along, too. I didn't like that because people would yell at her. "Look at her shoving and pushing!" "Don't you know where the end of the line is? Back there!" "Must be deaf!" "Where are you bulldozing your way to now? Hey, can't you hear?" Grandmama would hold my hand and drag me along and I couldn't see anything among the people because they'd be trying to squeeze me out, and Grandmama would be yelling, too: "Shameless creatures! Can't you see I have a child with me?" "You should have sent your maid!" "This lout she calls a child!" "Why didn't you leave him at home?" "In a white hat! She always wears a white hat when they're selling lard." Grandmama would tear the white hat off her head and everybody could see she was almost completely bald, and then we'd be served right away. Grandmama told me that one particular saleswoman cheated everybody and that her blond hair was dyed. Once, this saleswoman started to scream: "Oh! Oh my God!" She was flailing her arms, banging all over the place with her hands and screaming, "Ohmygod!" and stamping her feet. "Get out of here! All of you! Oh my God, why don't you all shut up! Or get out of here! I'm a working woman! I can't work like this! I can't count like this! I've got to keep track! I can't bear this! I can't stand it! I'll just stop, that's all! I can't stand it!" Everyone fell silent. She cut the lard with a huge knife and slapped it on a sheet of paper, and everybody kept quiet. She threw the paper on the scale and cut some more and smeared it on the paper again and watched the scale. She was crying. We were standing right up front. The woman went on cutting the lard and crying; she'd wipe her eyes and her face got all greasy and all we heard was her crying and the paper rustling. I was afraid we would be chased away. We put the fish into the bathtub. That night there was a knocking on my window. I didn't dare get out of bed even though I could see the army cap: it was my father. We put the fish in the sink so Father could take a bath. He soaped himself standing in the tub. When we were standing in the market, the woman with dyed blond hair couldn't go on weighing the lard. She stood there shaking, with the big knife in her hand, and crying. Then a man I recognized from church went around the counter to her. Grandmama said that when I got older I could be an altar boy, but Father shouldn't know about it, and then I could hold the little bell. Each time I shook the bell everybody would kneel. When we were all on our knees, this man who went behind the counter to the woman would look at us, I didn't understand why, I didn't do anything! and he put his arm around the woman and made her sit down on a box and started to console her. "Calm down! Calm down! Please, calm down! Everyone's being quiet now. You can do your work, keep count, nice and easy." We were kneeling and the bells began to toll in the tower, clanging and pealing. The priest raised his arms and showed us the body of the Lord. The woman kept crying and couldn't stop. We stood there, just looking at her. I liked to look at Father soaping himself, he could even do his back. The woman brought her hands together. She was shaking as if afraid of somebody. The long knife in her hand. "Don't be angry with me, please! I can't bear it! I can't bear it! Don't be angry with me!" The man I'd seen in church was stroking her dyed blond hair. "Please, calm down! Nobody's angry with you. We're all human beings." But then somebody said the man was comforting the woman only because he wanted to get his lard out of turn, and then everybody started shouting again. The fish kept opening its mouth, moving its gills, swimming around in the tub. Grandmama said we'd eat it on Friday. I pictured the image of the crucifix. The hammer, the pliers, the saw and nails were kept in a drawer in the hallway, under the mirror. I looked at my palm, but I didn't dare drive a nail into it. The fish was swimming as if looking for an exit. During a single round of the tub it opened its gills four times. Grandpapa asked me if I wanted to hear the story of the girl who smelled like a fish. "Yes." "Well, listen, then," Grandpapa said, "so you'll know what's what!" We were looking at the fish. "Everything in this story happened a very long time ago, and very far from here." I thought he meant the time of the ancestors he'd told me about up in the attic, but Grandpapa shook his head. "No! Didn't I ask you to listen? You're not paying attention! Our ancestors have had no time even to die, and they're still alive, they live here, within us. But the story I'm about to tell you happened in times we've already forgotten, when giant monsters, serpent-demons, dragons, and great ghosts were still living on earth; and they lived and loved and hated one another as humans do. All that's left now is love and hatred. Whenever you see a lizard or a snake, you see the shadow of monsters! think of that! And that's the time, the time of miracles, that I want to tell you about, and that's a very distant territory. A huge region. *Ein unübersehbares Gebiet*. Ancestors, that's a different time. They lived in the land of Haran, where Abraham came from, they lived in the land of Canaan, where Jacob escaped from, they lived in Egypt land, where Joseph became ruler, our ancestors lived in the valley of the Euphrates, in the Jordan valley, along the Nile, but that's right here, only an arm's length away; can't you hear it? the palm trees, the date palms rustling in the sweltering heat? feel the sand crunching between your teeth? not to mention the flowering olive groves of Cordova! or the fragrance of the German oak forests! they are all here, no need for long memories. But now I'm telling you about things you can't possibly remember. This is where I should have begun. Or even before. Maybe I should have started by saying that in the beginning God created heaven and earth. In the beginning, but when? And that is an unfathomable time, not only for you but for me, too. And out of what? Did the spirit create matter, and then matter created this comedy of the spirit? But even if I didn't start here, you would get to these areas by yourself. Well then, some time after the creation, which means a long time ago and far away, there lived a river, the great river, what kind of river? back then people didn't call rivers by names! but later it had a nickname—Ganga—and on the shore of this river there lived a heavenly fairy. And now the tale begins. Her hair was black as night, her eyes radiant like the surface of the water in the brightest hour, her skin smooth silk. And that's how the heavenly fairy lived, rejoicing in her own beauty. Not far from the river: a thick forest. There, where even the sunshine couldn't penetrate, in eternal dimness, nourishing his old body with grass and snakes, lived a saintly man. Mortal, but as pure in his saintliness as was the heavenly fairy in her beauty, as pure as a mortal could possibly be. He never felt desires, therefore he was never driven by hatred or love. An incurious being, a crystal of existence, a crystalline soul locked in perishable flesh. And the days of the flesh were numbered. The flesh was waiting for death, the flesh of the heart, the flesh of the stomach still digesting berries, the thin membranes, the walls of the veins all waiting to die. There, in the depth of the dark forest. Because where the hell else should a saint await death if not in the depth of the dark forest? That's what tales are like. Now he had only a few hours left. He knew that once these days, months, or hours were over, he would return his sensate body and insensate soul to the lap of the one infinite power. And when that happened, this soul would never again be born in flesh, in a mortal. He set out. But in the moonlight he saw the heavenly fairy bathing in the river. The girl's bottom was round, nice and round, as if a smooth round loaf were looking at itself in the mirror. Her two breasts are like two young roes that are twins, which feed among the lilies. The wise man, rooted to the spot, asked himself, Who is she that looketh forth as the morning, fair as the moon, clear as the sun, fragrant as springtide? And the wise man nearly cried out, saying, Whoever you are! Draw me, we will run after thee! But no words left his lips. Darkness burst into light! His seed spilled to the ground. The wise man understood: the former was desire, the latter gratification, feelings without which it had been his share to live all the days of his life. This is the enchanted filth that would defile me, so that I would be born to a new life, like vermin! And in his wrath he called down a curse upon the fairy. Be thou a mute fish! May you live in the water until you give birth to two children! Why this particular curse out of all possible curses? I don't know. The fairy plashed into the water. She lived among the fish. That beautiful mouth of hers was gaping like this fish's here." Grandmama came in: What's the delay with the fish? "Just finishing the story! She spent many years in the river. Maybe five thousand. But then, at dusk, a fisherman came, cast his net into the great water, and caught the beautiful little fish. He put the fish in his knapsack and took it home. To kill it, he knocked it on the head, just as I will knock this one in a minute. Cut open its stomach to clean out all the dirty innards. But look at this! The beautiful fish had no innards. Two tiny children were cowering in its belly. One was fashioned to be a little boy, the other one was a little girl. The fisherman was very scared and sent for the king. The king examined the signs, being well versed in such matters, and said, You and I are lucky, because spirit gives birth to spirit, even down to seven generations, and because this spirit chose to divide its immortality in two, we can share it. I'll take the boy with me and raise him. You take care of the girl, she is yours. And in two days the girl grew up and she was beautiful. Her hair black as night, her eyes radiant like the surface of the water in the brightest hour, her skin smooth silk. Still, she didn't have any suitors, because she smelled bad, like a fish. Every sentence is the setting for the jewel of wisdom! Are you listening? Pay close attention to this! The spirit, when it crawls into a body, becomes smelly! That's the meaning of the curse! But let's get quickly to the end of this, so you can hold the whole fruit in your hand. The fisherman let the girl work as a ferry woman. She took people back and forth across the river. The passengers were dazzled by her, but they couldn't touch her. Many years went by, but the girl was not getting old. What was she like after so very many years?" Grandpapa raised his finger. This meant I had to learn by heart what he was about to say. He also raised his fingers when he rattled off the seven cardinal sins. "Because of the seven sins God has withdrawn into the seventh heaven. Why? Come on! Tell me! Why?" "Because the serpent tempted Adam and Eve into the sin of pleasure. And God withdrew into the first heaven." "Go on!" "Because the sin of envy deprived Cain of his humanity and he murdered his own brother." "Who was he?" "Abel. And God withdrew into the second heaven." "Go on!" "Because Enoch and his companions fell into the sin of idolatry." "And God?" "Withdrew into the third heaven." "What do we call idolatry?" "When people worship not the Creator but His creations!" "What do we call God's creations?" "I don't know." "What do you mean you don't know? Think! You know everything! There's no such thing as 'I don't know'! Know then: God's creation includes everything that exists in heaven and on earth, in the known and the unknown world, and also everything that does not exist. Go on! Continue!" "Continue what?" "Noah's time is next!" "People in Noah's time were guilty of the sin of cruelty, and they were unworthy. And God withdrew into the fourth heaven. King Amraphel, wallowing in the sin of injustice, oppressed other peoples who had never harmed him. For this, God withdrew into the fifth heaven." "Why did he withdraw into the sixth?" "King Nimrod built a tower." "In Babylon. Why?" "Because he wanted to reach all the way up to heaven!" "And what's that?" "The sin of ambition!" "Finish the list of sins!" "And God was already looking at us from the sixth heaven because a king had taken from Abraham, who was formerly Abram, one of his wives, thus committing a sin against family happiness." Grandpapa wanted me to learn everything that he knew. Together we repeated: "Her hair black as night, her eyes radiant like the surface of the water in the brightest hour, her skin smooth silk." Grandpapa laughed, glad that I already knew the words, and he shouted, "That's what a beautiful woman is like! But let's hear what happened. A beautiful woman is beautiful even after a thousand years! A thousand years later a wise old man came to the river. The woman who smelled like fish was taking him across. It was the spirit that made her immortally beautiful, the spirit which, as we know, smells foul when inside a body. The wise man began pleading with her that she should gratify him when they reached the other side. But this is how the girl answered him: Lots of people live on the shore of the river, fishermen and hermits. You want me to love you right before their eyes? The wise man raised his finger and fog descended over the whole region. And the powerful old man was snickering under his beard at how quickly he had outsmarted the girl! But this is how the girl responded: I am pure as the snow at the peak of the highest mountain. If you soil my purity, what will be left for me? If a girl is not only beautiful but also clever, her tongue sharp as a hot paprika, she's all the more desirable! He let out a horrendous laugh, only the devil could laugh like that, making even the fish in the water break out in a cold sweat, that's how wickedly the old man was laughing. Perhaps you find me unattractive? He chuckled. True, my teeth have fallen out, but only because I don't need to chew any food. The hair in my ears grows like sedge in shallow water, but only because I don't need to hear any more sounds. The coating on my tongue turned blue a thousand years ago and my skin has not been soaked by the sweat of love for six hundred years, it is cracked like the earth, but how could I desire you so fervently if you are so obtuse that you cannot see past the body to my soul, stupid woman! your disgust reaches only my body! But the girl said, I can see your soul, old man. I see that your soul is ready for love, and I'm always ready to love your soul. This clever reply made the wise man's mind leap, frisking with pleasure. And this is what he said: If your soul is ready to love my soul, I promise only my soul will touch your body. So that you may see my strength, my power! And in the wink of an eye the old man turned into a strapping young man. Oh, God, how masterfully you have invented the duel of love! The fish-smelling girl, the clever one, had only one wish: that her body not smell like a fish. And she received him. At the spot where she received him she remained fish-smelling. On the same day she gave birth to Vyasa. And on the same day Vyasa matured into a lovely youth and asked his mother to leave him to himself, for having conquered the tyranny of the body, he would like to devote his life to God. The girl was left all alone, just as the saint in the forest had promised. She married one of the fishermen, became a woman like the rest of the girls, gave birth like the others, seven times, her breasts drooped, wrinkles invaded her lips, and she died. It was Vyasa who continued to live the life of the fairy which his grandmother had planted into his mother and his father had passed on to him. That's what the fairy tale tells us." "And is this true?" I asked. Grandmama was calling out that we should bring the fish. The fish was calmly swimming around the tub, not knowing what would happen to it if we took it to Grandmama. And when I asked Grandpapa what his grandfather was like, he didn't answer me. It was so dark in his eyes, no matter how hard I looked I couldn't see what was in them. I thought he would start shouting. When he shouted for a long time his mouth went black. But he only raised his finger: "The time has come!" And he looked at me as if he were searching for something in me. And slowly he laid his hand back on the armrest of his chair. With its fingers open the hand rested on the maroon velvet. As if it were not a hand but a strange animal. Sometimes I would touch the thick veins. While he was asleep. "Put your hand on my head." He was whispering. His hair was soft and white. I didn't understand. He gave me a look and then lowered his lids. A vein was bulging on his white temple, too; once, on a map, he'd shown me what a winding and twisting river the Jordan was. My hand became warm on his head. He was whispering: "The time has come! I can see it. Your mind is opening up to the idea of time. I can see it. And that's a great thing. Let's help with the opening of the gates, shall we?" He was nodding, and gave me a nice smile, and opened his eyes and pressed me to his chest. "Help me get up!" But I couldn't help him, because he was hugging me, and I saw from very close the little pores on his nose, full of little specks of dirt which I had never noticed before. I thought he was going to cry and then I would see from this close where the tears were coming from, but he yelled and I could see into his mouth. "Help me get up!" But I couldn't help him. "Give me my stick!" While I was looking for his stick, Grandpapa held on to the chair, though he could walk even without his stick. Grandpapa was very large. When he got up it seemed the room wouldn't be big enough for him. The walls came closer. He was walking with his stick, and he was yelling, "The time has come!" But I didn't understand and had no idea where he was going and didn't follow him because I was a little afraid, but at the door he turned around and yelled, "Why don't you open the door for me?" I opened the door for him. "We're going upstairs." We were walking in the mirror, Grandpapa and I. Slowly up the stairs. Grandpapa was in a hurry. The steps were creaking. Resting after each step. While resting he breathed fast, but as if something was in his throat. Which wouldn't let the air out. "Before I die." I thought he wanted to show me something, like pictures. "Just in time." Grandmama wasn't at home, because she'd gone to the market to see what she could buy. That's when she bought the fish. Whenever Grandmama left the house Grandpapa would think of something to do. On top of the stairs we rested for a long time. We didn't go to Grandpapa's old room, and we had already passed Grandmama's room. That's where Grandmama listened to the radio. When they took the armchair downstairs because Grandpapa couldn't climb the stairs any more, Father said he'd take the radio downstairs, too, but Grandpapa said he didn't need it, he wasn't interested in lies. "You'll completely lose touch with life like that, Father!" "From now on that is exactly my task! To lose touch!" And at the end of the upstairs corridor was the steel door with the big key. "Open it!" Grandpapa said. "Are we going to the attic?" We sat on the broken sofa. Where I'd sat with Csider. "Sit next to me so you won't see my face." And he didn't say anything more. I thought we'd have a quiet time just thinking about things. Our shoes in the dust. He was breathing hard in the heat. I was afraid, I didn't know what might happen. And everything was rather dim, and the roof tiles were making little crackling sounds, and Grandpapa was breathing, and above our heads the sun shone through the window, but I couldn't see the sky, only the light as it was falling, slanted and never-ending, into the attic. I didn't know what could possibly be happening to Grandpapa's face that I wasn't allowed to see and yet I had to stay there. Just keep sitting together. Grandmama always cleaned Grandpapa's yellow shoes and brushed them till they shone brightly. Maybe I'd have to tell him again what I was thinking about, but I didn't know what I was thinking, and I wasn't allowed to say I didn't know, but I really didn't know. I would have liked to stamp my feet on the floor, the attic had a strange hollow sound. In the attic I could feel the house under me, yet it was like not being in the house. With a long stick I poked at the dim, dark corners. Before I'd settle in one, let other creatures get out. By the time I turned my head in their direction they disappeared. Gone behind my back. I could see their color, like the dust of the attic: gray. They were crouching at the foot of the beams or standing by the chimney. When I came with the stick they seemed about to scream, they opened their mouths and vanished. Always getting behind my back. Once, when I turned to see where one of them had disappeared to, and spun around so fast it wouldn't have time to scurry away, it was hanging on the rope off a beam because it had hanged itself, and its skin had already dried and stuck to its bones, or maybe it was like that all the time, but then it disappeared, too. Grandpapa was breathing slowly, but his forehead was sweaty, and he sat all doubled up and his eyes were closed, as if he had fallen asleep. "Don't look at me!" I can't imagine how he could have seen me with his eyes shut. "When I was a child, we sat down on the bench in my grandfather's courtyard. Under the mulberry tree. Don't look at me! said my grandfather, just listen to what I'm about to tell you. My face must not interfere with your vision." I watched the light falling between the rafters and the motes undulating. "I leaned back against the trunk of the mulberry tree, taking care my grandfather didn't see this little impropriety, and I looked up into the leaves, each leaf separately; so many leaves! Occasionally a mulberry would plunk down. We settled on that bench because I asked my grandfather what his grandfather had been like, and then my grandfather said the time has come and made me sit on the bench. It was Sabbath, that is, Saturday, after lunch. For lunch we had cholent, the bean dish baked overnight in the home kiln, with fine, tender beef in it, and we also had sweet hominy, served cold. By the time my grandfather finished with everything I'm about to tell you now, the evening star had risen in the clear sky. But we kept on sitting there for a long time and saw the full moon, too, and it was red. My grandfather said he would be embarrassed if he couldn't begin what he wanted to tell me the way his grandfather had started his story. And his grandfather had also said he would be embarrassed if he couldn't begin his story the way his grandfather had begun his. And it began like this: you are a kohen, from the family of the high priest Aaron, which means nothing more and nothing less than as if I had said—and this is what my grandfather said to me and his grandfather had said to him—that you are one of the chosen group within the chosen people, the brother of Moses, the man whom God addressed thus, according to Scripture: And thou shalt speak unto all that are wise-hearted, whom I have filled with the spirit of wisdom, that they make Aaron's garments to consecrate him, that he may minister unto Me in the priest's office. Thus my grandfather's grandfather had quoted the words to him, and thus he quoted the words to me, as I am quoting the words to you, and that is how they opened the gate which I am opening for you now. Do you hear what I am saying? Because speaking this softly I cannot hear my own words, I can only feel them. If a deaf man speaks softly it's as if not he but his spirit were speaking. Right now, like this, all right?

Can you still hear me like this?" "Yes, I can." "That's the answer I gave my grandfather, too. Under the mulberry tree, on the bench. His grandfather had come here from Nicolsburg. The courtyard was small, sitting on the bench you could see the snow-capped mountains. In clear weather, over the stone fence. The stone fence stank, still we liked to play there. No matter how hard my grandmother had tried to chase them away, the drunks came to urinate by the stone fence. My grandfather sold wine and spirits, but he also sold oil, salt, thread, candles, sugar, and fabrics. For fine fabrics he would go to Vienna, Berlin, or Budapest. Of course it was more for the books and good conversation that he traveled so far. He'd bring back two bolts of material. One was dark green, the other dark brown. It took him about a year to sell both. Then he could get on the road again. Once, from Vienna, he brought a parasol for Grandmother; it was mauve, or rather, cyclamen-colored. Grandmother wrapped it up nicely and put it in the closet. Some years later somebody remembered: Why doesn't Mrs. Simon use the parasol her husband brought her? Grandmother was surprised. What would people say if a Jewish woman walked around in the village on weekdays with a parasol? And on Saturday I'm not going anywhere, because the Lord has sanctified the Sabbath. But my grandfather had read so much that he began to doubt whether there was a God. The courtyard, at the center of which stood the mulberry tree, was surrounded by this stone fence, and the store opened from there, not from the street. Very clever. If something should happen, it wouldn't be so easy to loot it. It was the grandfather who had come here from Nicolsburg who figured this out. In case something happened they could lock and bolt the gate. From the store you could go into the living room. That's where Grandfather sat with his books, in front of the window. I can still see it today. If anybody came, I can still hear the little door in the front gate, and then the little bell on the store door would ring, and Grandfather would call out from behind his book, telling the customer to take what he liked, just leave the money on the counter. Go on, pour for yourself, drink. But this didn't work too well because a lot of people cheated him. And Grandmother's counting and recounting the pennies didn't help much; Grandfather was going quite mad with his learning and yelling that he couldn't be bothered with oil and salt until he clarified for himself the existence of God. This is understandable! He would eat and rest only to gather the further strength needed to unlock the mystery of mysteries. And if he was working on the mystery of mysteries, how could they expect him to pour drinks for inebriated peasants? That's understandable! Well, isn't it? Grandmother understood, all right, but she pulled asunder what God had put together: the great conjugal bed. So long as he is wallowing in the sin of being a nonbeliever, so long as he refuses to take care of the store, he cannot touch me! I don't want his sins to be paid for by those who haven't even been conceived! The rabbi agreed with Grandmother, but he also wasn't angry with Grandfather. He told Grandmother it would be best to wait. That's how they continued to live together. For eight years no more children were born. They already had three. But eight years later Grandfather found the irrefutable arguments. And in the ninth year my father was born. Your father was born, the firstborn of my own faith, the one and only, my real son, my Joseph, the son conceived in the bliss of faith. That's how Grandfather said it under the mulberry tree, and we could already see the evening star in the sky, this sentence was the period at the end of his narrative, and then the moon rose, all red. But Grandfather, your great-great-grandfather, could not have known then what I, your grandfather, know now. He couldn't have known that the doubt germinating in him for eight years would grow ears, shoot up, and ripen in me, ready to be harvested; I couldn't have known this either when the red moon rose that evening. Though that, too, must have been a signal. What in him was only a doubt, in me turned into certainty. I couldn't have known then that I was coming into the world to carry out the law, to bring about destiny, and to guide the great river back to the place from which two thousand years ago it had set out to meander all over the world. I have to utter a single word which I wouldn't want to say. Jesus. Once, in 1598, one of your ancestors in Buda cried out like this: Let us die so that we may be saved. That has become my motto. You too will have to choose a motto, or it might choose you. To kill everything that has remained so that we may go on living! Kill it, so all this can turn into a dead myth. Because a savior was born, but the people did not notice. Only the punishment their inattention would bring upon them. For the Law, the Torah, says it very clearly: But if thou will not hearken unto the voice of the Lord thy God, cursed shalt thou be in the city, and cursed shalt thou be in the field. Cursed shall be thy basket and thy store. Cursed shall be the fruit of thy body, and the fruit of thy land, the increase of thy kine, and the flocks of thy sheep. Cursed shalt thou be when thou comest in, and cursed shalt thou be when thou goest out. The Lord shall make the pestilence cleave unto thee. And thou shalt grope at noonday, as the blind gropeth in darkness; and thou shalt not prosper in thy ways; and thou shalt be only oppressed and spoiled evermore, and no man shall save thee. And the Lord shall scatter thee among people which neither thou nor thy fathers have known, and there thou shalt serve other gods: even wood and stones. The curse! I have turned the curse into my life! That is why I have come. To fulfill the curse! Red was the moon that rose then! To die so that we may be saved! That is why I have come, to fulfill the curse, the final devastation. That's why I planted my own seed in a Christian woman and shared the blood; but your father took a Jewess for himself and thus in you he squandered what I had gained, your blood is more Jewish again; but you too will take Christian blood to yourself, and in this way the Jewish blood will dwindle away! This is what I have come to fulfill! To kill, for life! For the blood must not be allowed to dwindle; what once was, still is. If only a single drop of it is left in a thousand years, that drop will be there, in someone. A single drop. You don't understand! Of course, you cannot understand, for you cannot enter through this gate any more, your blood has been mixed, it cannot carry you in, only close enough to take a look inside. But do look inside. Let us begin where my grandfather began. Listen! We sat down on the bench. And this is how my grandfather spoke: Why did God pick Aaron to be His priest, why Aaron? Only because he was an eloquent speaker? No point looking for the answer in Aaron. One hundred, two hundred, maybe four hundred years earlier, and where was Aaron then? That's where you find the explanation: and not anywhere else but on Leah's lips. When that love-starved ugly female, that loyal bitch, was made pregnant for the second time by Jacob, and on the morrow she cried out joyously, like this: Because the Lord hath heard me! And she gave birth to her son and she called his name Simeon, which means, having been heard. Just as the Lord had given the son into Leah's womb, so did the Lord put the son's name unto her lips. And that is the first seal. For this name, Simon or, more archaically, Simeon, has a double meaning, and the two are woven together; one of its meanings is, The bearer of the name will hear the voice of the Lord; its other meaning is, The Lord will hear the voice of the one entitled to this name. And what happens when someone breaks the seal of the name, like Leah's second son, who in his heedlessness did not hear the Lord? Leah's son wrought terrible, bloody vengeance on the inhabitants of Shechem after they had defiled Dinah. He took revenge on the innocent because the guilty ones had run away. And that was a sin! And the Lord avenged the sin with a curse—so that they shall remember! And He delivered Simeon and his tribe into servitude, into the hands of their own brethren. That is the second seal. That's how the Simons become servants, if only God's servants. That is the third seal. And six thousand years have gone by. And since that time this has been your name. But the gate is not quite open yet, there is only a slight crack but it's widening. Don't look at me! Just listen! I'm going on with the story."

"At that time there lived two Simons in Jerusalem. One of them got there only a few months earlier, at the beginning of Nisan, but when his master was crucified because he'd declared himself the Messiah, King of the Jews, this Simon was stuck there for a while. Sometimes, after sundown, he would be seen going through the city gate, but nobody knew where he was headed or whether he was leaving for good. And those who knew kept their peace. But he was watched. The other Simon came from Cyrene; his sons were born in Jerusalem, where he lived for many years. These two Simons did not know each other, only heard of each other—I do have a relative in Jerusalem, one would say, originally from faraway Cyrene, but I don't know him personally; and the other one knew this much, I do have a relative somewhere in Galilee, where he was a fisherman until he met this false prophet who for the last three years has been roaming around unpunished, dazzling the gullible multitudes with his miracles, until this charlatan told him, From henceforth thou shalt be a fisher of men, and took him on as his disciple, and who knows where they are now, that's what people have told me. The two Simons had never seen each other, though the Lord saw to it that a particular day, the fifteenth of Nisan, was a memorable one for both of them. They resembled each other, both in appearance and in their nature, as if the same mother had given birth to them; they were both short, gaunt, with burning dark eyes, and extremely taciturn. Those who knew them only casually could easily take one for the other. Look! Here comes Simon of Galilee, the disciple of the one whose name is not to be uttered, and how rich a garment he's wearing today, what magnificent sandals! Look, here he comes! Could this be Simon of Cyrene? But why the shabby garb, what garbage dump did he get his torn sandals from? The two Simons were not looking for each other. One was as rich as the other was poor. And each said to himself when thinking of the other, What have I got to do with him? That was a mistake. But who can comprehend his own mistakes? The Lord had some problems with them, but until He arranged for them to meet, almost two thousand years had to go by. Not a long time. They met in me. But I won't say anything about that for now. My grandfather couldn't have known about this, and now I can tell you only what he told me on the bench under the mulberry tree. Those two couldn't meet because Simon of Galilee, who was under the Sanhedrin's surveillance, took untrodden paths and gave wide berth to the abodes of the rich; he would disappear for days, they'd lose track of him, and then he would suddenly reappear in a dark doorway or in the midday shade of an alley, and the spies would resume their trailing, like dogs. The two Simons were not allowed to meet; the Lord deferred their meeting to a later date, they couldn't meet because while Simon of Galilee, fisher of men, took to strange roads, the other Simon, the rich one from Cyrene, to whom that memorable thing happened on the fifteenth of Nisan, a Friday, this Simon, when the eight days of Passover were over and everything in Jerusalem returned to its usual, everyday routine, this Simon locked himself up for good in his own house. Crouching in a dark hot room, he waited for the news and prayed a lot. When addressed he wouldn't answer, he barely touched his food, and a frightened silence ruled his entire house. Of his children he loved Alexander most, his older son, the firstborn. He loved Alexander even though the boy showed no signs that he could continue his father's pursuits; this boy knew nothing about money, had no idea what to buy and when, or how to sell at a profit; only the farmland held Alexander's interest, the way plants grew and animals were born; but this love of the land was still dearer to the father's eyes and heart than the tinkering of Rufus, the younger boy, who even as a small child would stand for hours in front of the workshops of gold- and silversmiths, watching them pound out their trays and pitchers, absorbed in the adroit movements with which they fit precious stones into ornaments to be worn on necks, hands, and feet. It was already the middle of the month of Iyar. People were quickly forgetting that someone had been crucified. Alexander harvested the barley from which the first sheaf would be part of the holiday sacrifice; the barley that year had a twentyfold yield, twenty seeds for every seed planted, which could be called a good average. The hot days were already ripening the wheat. But Simon cared for none of this. He couldn't step out of the house because the light hurt his eyes, and he no longer knew where this light was coming from or what it really was; the city's noise offended his ears, and if he had to mingle with the people jostling around the temple, who were so filthy and ignorant, he would have felt that everybody was looking at him and mocking him; Simon prayed, asking the Lord to enlighten his mind so that he might understand what was happening. Sometimes he would call for Alexander—the boy could not see his father in the dark—and ask him to go to the temple and inquire of Rabbi Abiathar if there was any news, but the rabbi's message was always the same: Nothing. Simon was lost in this nothingness. Within a few days he was found dead. Instead of feeling bereaved, Rufus was annoyed. While looking at his dead father he thought, We found him dead in the corner, like a dog. He went up on the roof, along the edge of which ran a wide carved stone balustrade and handsome columns supported a light shade against the sun—that was all the fashion in Jerusalem, but some thought it was a loathsome aping of the Romans, and as such deeply immoral: to block the light from our faces! thus, allegedly, grumbled Rabbi Abiathar himself—when he leaned on the stone balustrade, Rufus sometimes could see, on the shadeless roof of the neighboring house, the girl he loved and with whom the Lord would bring him together on the fifteenth of Nisan, the day that had proved so fateful for his father. And now he desired to see her more than ever before, because from now on he could love not only the proportions of her body, the sheen of her hair, and her awkward side glances, but also the fragrance of her breath, her voice, her fearful alarm, and her laughter. On the death day, the girl did not show. A mulberry fell on my grandfather's forehead. I didn't dare laugh, even though he smeared it all over his face. He always felt and knew everything. He said, Don't look! If you look, you can't listen, and a mulberry is no big thing." Quickly I turned my head because I also caught myself looking at Grandpapa. "That reminds me! To give you an idea what my grandfather was like! Once we were playing under the mulberry tree and the mulberries kept falling off the tree, and we made up a word game. Mulberry in Hungarian is *szeder*, which sounds like Seder, so we made up the song: The szeder tree burst into bloom on Seder eve! Seder-bloom the eveburst bloomszeder intotree! Szederburst treeve sederinto! Evetree on bloominto sederburst! Der evenszeder burst bloome in der sedtree! And we ran to Grandfather and asked him, DER EVENSZEDER BURST BLOOME IN DER SEDTREE—what does that mean? Grandfather laughed. *Ihr seid ja dumme Esel! Wir hatten dasselbe Spiel gemacht, als mein Grossvater diesen Baum setzte. Es ist ja ungarisch gesagt und heisst,** THE SEDER TREE BURST INTO BLOOM ON SZEDER EVE! Grandfather laughed and we were yelling and shouting, so happy that Grandfather knew everything but had gotten it mixed up, and we shouted, *Nein! Nein! Eben umgekehrt!* Just the opposite! ON SEDER EVE THE

* You are asses! We used to play that game when my grandfather planted this tree. It's Hungarian, and it means . . .

SZEDER TREE BURST INTO BLOOM!" Grandpapa laughed. I was glad because I also knew one of these word plays. "Grandpapa, I've got one, too!" Grandpapa did not respond, but I went ahead anyway: "PATYA RATYA TYATYA RA ARA TYATYA TYARA PA! You know what that means?" Grandpapa was quiet. I was looking down at his shoes, but not even his shoes moved. I didn't know why he didn't laugh, why he didn't respond, why he didn't like it, and there was such a silence, and in the silence the flies were buzzing and I could still hear the stupid thing I'd just said, and it was Gábor who learned this from somebody in school, and it had to be said really fast. "Nobody knows, Grandpapa, because it doesn't make any sense, it doesn't mean anything." I was looking at his yellow shoes in the dust. "That day, Thursday, the fourteenth day of Nisan, Rufus did not see Rachel on the roof. Do you hear what I am saying, do you? Listen! Rufus is a very handsome youth. His body is well-proportioned, smooth and glistening. Before leaving the house or going up on the roof he carefully oils his body and combs his hair. He's satisfied with nothing less well-proportioned than he is himself. But since he believes himself to be more shapely than he is, he's dissatisfied with most things. While up on the roof, leaning against the balustrade and waiting for Rachel to appear on the neighboring rooftop, Rufus sees his mother down in the courtyard coming in with two servants carrying the paschal lamb; she stops in the shade and, raising her hand to her forehead, softly calls up to her son: Rufus, please put on some decent clothes today! Rufus leans against a column, doesn't answer. He runs his finger across the stone, his fingers like the feel of the finely carved fluting. The clothes Rufus wears are not like his grandfather's, or his father's, or even his brother's. Rufus dresses according to the latest fashion: a white, light wrap, gathered and held in rich folds on one shoulder by an ornamental clasp; he himself made the clasp and fitted it with precious stones. He's also made the belt, which shows his slender waist as even narrower than it is. The garb is short, exposing not only one of his shoulders on top but also his well-formed knees, his shapely thighs and powerful legs, it's that short. The garb is elegant, but it also has a martial air; legionnaires wear something similar. In the motionless air the city is boiling. From here you can see the city wall and the Southern Gate, where groups of arrivals set up camp, stir up the dust. The sun is still in the sky, but the noise is increasing, because as soon as the sun sets the killing of lambs will begin all over the city. The eight-day holiday is about to commence in Jerusalem. Newcomers are looking for lodging, a courtyard where they might set up their tents. Word has it that during the night, at the head of a whole legion, Pilate had also come to town. For the skin of a lamb one can get lodging. Up on the roof, above the throng and the hubbub, Rufus feels himself more of an outsider than the poorest beggar. He believes this to be so because of his love, which nothing can assuage. But no! The roots of his love are sickly. It's not a wife he wants to take according to the Law, but, rather, he wants to possess beauty, to capture the elusive in the palpable. And what is taking place around him, below him, is so chaotic and coarse, so against his liking. Rachel, who in the company of her mother and sisters sometimes appears on the neighboring roof, is slender, yet her body is also round. The contrast of her slenderness, a sign of upward striving, and her roundness, the body's tendency to curve back onto itself, makes for a perfect shape, and that is what is driving Rufus on: his eyes are enjoying in the girl the same perfection that he manages to mold with his hands, with his fine little chisels and hammers, when making filigrees of silver or copper. And he finds this play of opposites in his own unclothed body, a sin which is no secret to his parents; his mother often spies on him and what she sees—though she finds the words with great difficulty—she relates to Simon. Proportions! In Jerusalem everything is governed by laws, but the laws are proportioned differently; the mind's rule over the senses, reason, not the rule of faith! and reason without the senses is disproportionate! In law it's logic that keeps the right proportions, and everything that falls out of the realm of the law's logic is filth, waste! A sense or feeling that begs to take tangible form is considered a disrespectful violation of the law! The lamb that one must slaughter after sundown but before darkness falls must be a yearling and a male; and that evening everywhere the meal, dedicated to the memory of a people's flight, must be consumed in haste, without enjoyment; to eat the lamb's blood is forbidden, it's a sin! You must not break its bones! Any member of the family who partakes not of the paschal meal, of the lamb and of the bitter herbs, partakes of death! For he has sinned! It's a sin! The next morning Rufus may again wear his fancy clothes. Today is the fifteenth of Nisan, that day. On the second day of Pesach let every man who harvests his own land bring a sheaf of first fruits for a temple offering! Rufus takes the sickle, Alexander brings the sheaf, and stepping smartly in front of them is their father, who is much shorter than they. Their land is outside the city, beyond the Northern Gate. Now they're coming back. Simon is silent, his sons are not talking either. The descent is steep from the bald rocky hilltop which, for this reason, people call Golgotha. In the hazy light past the valley of Kidron the Mount of Olives is shimmering. They keep going in silence even when they notice that something is happening down there, near the gate. The overheated morning light melts the bodies pouring out of the stone gate into one huge mass; the throng is flowing upward, the dark maw of the gate thrusting the waves of humanity into the light, into clouds of dust. Soldiers' armor, tips of lances sparkle in the sun. Simon stops, his sons stop. They're still far away, but they're defenseless. Simon gestures and they move to the side of the road and wait, motionless. Simon glances at Rufus. He's thinking about this road being the one on which his ancestors were led away into captivity. Simon does not love this son, even his reputedly ugly daughters he loves more, still he'd like to lighten Rufus's fate. To be so beautiful is simply senseless and difficult. The secret reports have filled him with trepidation. When Rufus was born—the second one's a boy, too!—Simon had laughed, he was so happy; it was a boy, his head covered with long red hair. That's why they called him Rufus, which means ruddy-headed. But Rufus's hair, as if rebelling even against its own name, has turned black. This is the road! says Simon, prompted by an educating impulse. This is the road on which the Babylonians drove our ancestors into captivity. I'm telling you, Rufus, so that you know! Freedom is a thorny thing. These days, like today, were sanctified by the Lord, may His name be blessed, and on days like these, law-abiding men look to their past, not at their own bodies. I am telling you both so that you may remember! This road guards the footsteps of those who return! In freedom the body tends to forget its own past. It's still not clear, they can't see what sort of crowd is clambering up the steep road. The fresh air is alive with the song of larks, but the roar propelling the endless crowd toward them can already be heard clearly, as if the earth were rumbling; they are coming closer and closer. The three of them are standing still, waiting. None of them speaks. Children are racing ahead. Naked striplings. Panting up the hill. Simon and his two sons are sucked into the din; a grotesque lunatic is hopping, flitting about, screeching and squawking like a bird; the pounding of feet. Upward rolls the cloud of dust, pulling the crowd into itself. Faster! Let's go! Inside a ring of soldiers three men stripped naked are gasping; the waist cloths have slipped to the side, no longer covering their loins, and sweat draws stripes across their bodies, following the traces of flogging; they're dragging their crosses on their shoulders, blood oozing from the shoulders, bruised flesh flashing bright; the pointed bottoms of the crosses grate, jump on the stones, bump into one another; the clicking and snapping of sandals. I can't! Come on! Screaming, the people shove and push the people at the head of the procession; everybody wants to see everything, and the soldiers are also helpless, maybe they even enjoy a little a confusion and turmoil which for once they don't have to quell. Simon looks at Rufus, and his voice, as always when addressing his son, is instructive. Sinners! he says softly, and repeats, Sinners! The officer in charge—the effects of his morning exercises cancelled out by days of voluptuous indulgence—is tired now, out of breath. He, who's supposed to be running things here, he too is being shoved along by the filthy mob. How do you know, Father? Rufus asks, offended by the paternal tone. How do you know? You were there when they committed their sins? Simon's eyes cloud with fury. The beautiful mouth is sharply insolent and tops off the words with a smile. When the officer glances at Simon their eyes lock, two raging beasts. The officer pumps as much air into his lungs as he can, and Simon is about to cry out when the officer shouts over the noise: Halt! A peaked helmet and a drenched, disgustingly clean-shaven Roman face flash through the clouds of fury darkening Simon's face. With a protective, haughty gesture Simon raises a hand to his chest. As if to say, What have I got to do with you? The officer doesn't know yet what he wants. Simon can smell the unpleasant odor rising from the other's body. Shalom! says the officer, peace be with you, grinning, but Simon does not reciprocate, which is a great insult, for the Roman has learned Aramaic well. The jumble of sounds subsides; the silence of the crowd is heavy and ominous, which surely means that something must happen now. You know who is going by here? Do you know who we have here? asks the officer, and smiles, glad to be able to catch his breath. In case you don't, I'll tell you. Your king! A curtained palanquin carried by four blacks is now lowered, it creaks. Simon thinks the officer's question and statement must refer to the person in the palanquin. But the palanquin's curtain is of cheap gauze. The King of the Jews in that! The lunatic squawks like a coupling dove. The Roman is shouting because he feels the approving murmurs are about to get out of hand. From the side of the road you're watching your king carrying his cross, is that what you're doing? Simon does not understand, he wants to back away, but the crowd is pushing, everybody wants to see everything, and he can no longer see his two sons, he's cut off and surrounded. I say to you, honorable Jew, you should carry his cross for him, after all he's your king! That's my opinion. A ripple of grating, indecent guffaws. Only those who know Simon dare not laugh. Should he carry it? the Roman bellows. The crowd responds in unison. I won't, Simon cries out, piercingly. But the mob keeps insisting, chanting rhythmically. They bump against Simon. And the procession moves on. For an instant, while he is being pushed and shoved about, he catches the eye of the naked man in the middle—he registers not the eyes, only the flash of the glance—and when he prays in his hot dark room, waiting to hear what the Sanhedrin and Rabbi Abiathar think of the unfolding events, when in his prayer he begs the Lord to enlighten him about the meaning of these events, then, in the great choking darkness, from time to time the light of this glance flashes up before him, but he does not understand, though light shineth in darkness, his darkness comprehendeth it not, this is the light he should cling to, this one, but he does not understand and prays to the Lord to be enlightened, and while doing so he fails to notice the light, the light of that countenance which the Lord had sent him. Oh, Lord, oh, God, if only I had been the Simon of that day! And that was the last warning. Pay heed, the world has changed! But Simon, son of *kohanim*, from the family of Aaron, comprehended it not. In the weight of the cross he felt not the burden of the warning but only the humiliation did he feel, poor man, and therefore he ran to the Law, to Rabbi Abiathar. Complaining. But what could Rabbi Abiathar tell him, as he rolled his parchment scrolls on their ebony rods? That's why I'm telling you, In every weight placed on you you must feel not only the burden, the humiliation, woe unto you if you cannot comprehend the burdens of the Lord! Don't suffer! Only the filthy beast in you suffers! Suffering is a burden, and the burden is a warning, an exhortation. You must rejoice in it! A warning. Everything is a warning about something! The day on the road in the forest of Saalfeld when that German spat on me and kicked me, and lying on the ground I was suffering the greatest of all humiliations, of not being able to die! then I also saw that light that was shining in my darkness. For the Lord had sent it again. He sent me what he had sent to Simon one thousand nine hundred and eleven years earlier. That's when the Lord linked me up, there, on that horseshit-covered road in Saalfeld, with those two Simons of yore. Because I seized what one of those Simons rejected. I seized what the other Simon seized nineteen hundred and eleven years earlier. That's how the two Simons were united in me. And I knew that death was not my fate, because I had died when I was born, and my death, when I die, will be followed by my life. That's why I'm not looking forward to death, but neither do I fear it. And what could Grandfather possibly have known of all this? What could he have known on that bench under the mulberry tree? What? But let's get back to where we were! We're in, inside the gate already! Come on! Don't look at me! Come, push along with me. We left off with Rufus struggling forward with his sickle, following his father, whom he cannot see. He is shoved and pushed by the people climbing up the hill, and he has to be careful with the sickle. And then he sees the girl whose bodily perfection his hands long to touch, then he sees Rachel—a very beautiful name, Rachel: it means mother sheep, a ewe. Rolling, crunching stones under the running feet. Rachel is running, frightened, looking for somebody, probably someone she's been separated from; but it's Rufus her eyes find. Raising the sickle above his head, pushing with his shoulders and treading on feet, Rufus makes his way to her. With his free hand he grabs Rachel's hand, presses this miracle of delicate little bones, soft flesh, and hot skin, he yanks her and pulls her along after him until they manage to tear themselves away from the crowd. At the side of the road he lets go of the hand that has nearly melted in their common sweat, but the sickle—so flustered, poor thing!—he's still holding above his head. The rabble surges on, is blocked, backs up, then resumes its push forward, the rear brought up by stragglers trying to keep up: the blind and the lame. Last of all is a leper who, as he's supposed to, keeps shouting as he races forward on his rotting feet: I'm a leper! Leper! And then the road empties out, turns white in the dazzling light. Murmuring noise from the top of the hill. Larks can be heard again, as though their song had never stopped. And the two of them are just standing there. Beautiful, isn't it? Isn't it? Of course this is not exactly the way my grandfather told me the story. He couldn't have known what I know now. But I've kept thinking about it and I've come to the conclusion that this is the only way it could have happened. Accurate memory helped me in this. All my grandfather said was that in Jerusalem there lived a Simon who had two sons. One of them, whom they called Rufus because he was a redhead at birth, took for his wife the beautiful Rachel and went to live in Rome. Because at the time one of Rachel's uncles lived in Rome. He had a big house, and many merchants worked for him. One of the merchants, who had spent Pesach in Jerusalem, told the uncle that Rufus, now a member of the family, fashioned pretty jewelry—rings, bracelets, pendants. The next year, when another merchant went to Jerusalem, the uncle sent a letter to the family: Glory be to the name of the Lord, my dear brethren, whom I wish to inform you, in case you haven't heard—which I doubt—that the clouds have passed over Rome and the sun is now shining brightly. It is true that the emperor, who fell victim of his own excesses, installed statues of himself in our synagogue, desecrating the temple with his body—lustful even when carved in marble—this being only one of his many sins! but the rabbis are wise! One Friday, in secret, they had a decorative hanging drawn around the statues, and thus we here in Rome, who worship the God you worship in Jerusalem, managed, thanks to the rabbis' wisdom, to avoid a mortal sin. Now, as I have said, the sun is shining. The statues were taken out of the temple and smashed to smithereens. It was hard, hard work, it took us three days just to break off the emperor's head. The new emperor, Claudius by name, not only has had all the statues destroyed but, thanks be to God, is also doing a thorough job of upsetting the old order; what was true only yesterday is not necessarily going to be true tomorrow; the confusion is complete; that's how it happens that he is now returning to us

—whom the old order had humiliated because of our faith—those rights and privileges which our ancestors enjoyed under Caesar and Augustus. Come to Rome, my dear brethren! Rome is a city hungry for beauty, and as I hear, Rufus, whom I don't yet know, beauty is no stranger to you. The altar fittings need repair, and every Roman lady wants Jewish jewelry. My house is big. I appreciate and value highly the ring you have sent me. I am sending you one, too, though compared to your gift, I know, it's inferior work. But accept it as a symbol—as our ancestors were wont to do—for with this ring I have made you my children, you poor, dear orphans. That's what the letter said. They embarked in the new port city of Caesarea, built by Herod the Great. The ship sailed to Cyprus. From there they headed to Crete, but for three days they were tossed about in a storm and on the fourth their ship crashed against a rock near the shores of Rhodes. On his back Rufus dragged Rachel ashore; in the meantime her first birth pangs began. That's where she gave birth to her son. They called him Caiaphas, which means rock or cliff. All their valuables were lost at sea. Rufus worked in Rhodes for a whole year and with the money he earned they continued their voyage. They reached Syracuse, but by then they had nothing to eat and little Caiaphas was whimpering. But many pious Jews lived there among the goyim and when they learned who Rachel's uncle was they gladly lent them money against a letter of credit. And so with no further mishaps the family arrived in Rome. Of course the uncle could not have known that one third of Simon of Cyrene's wealth would be swallowed up by the Pamphylian Sea, and that he would be stuck with some of the debts the newcomers had run up on the way. They were given a small room in the big house, but they were glad because the little room opened into the atrium, like all the others, and in the middle of the atrium a fountain was bubbling quietly. In this house Rachel gave birth to a girl, whom they called Yael, or wild goat that skips about on the hard rocks. The uncle was laughing behind the backs of his poor relatives: the ewe gave birth to a wild goat? Wonder who covered her? Caiaphas grew up to be beautiful, as his father had once been, but his beauty was soft, like his mother's before she had her children. At night he'd seek out the company of Macedonian slaves and hang around the theater; he knew how to imitate and mimic everybody, could sing and dance; in the end he disappeared, and people said he'd become an actor, but unfortunately not just an actor. Yael lived up to her name, too. Nobody knows where or when, but a youth from a prominent family fell in love with her. The young gentleman's name was Caius, a very popular name among Romans. He was proud not of his family but of his name. It was the same as that of Caius Marius, who was elected consul seven times because, allegedly, as a child he had found an eagle's nest with seven cheeping eaglets in it; and Julius Caesar was also Caius, Caius Julius Caesar, who was a relative of the great Marius, and therefore, to some extent, related to me, too; though they did not know each other, Caius was part of another, the next generation; but already in his early youth Caius took Marius as his model, the Marius who, as I've said, is my relative! Our stupid little Caius chose as models the two great ones so that, by holding forth about them, his own insignificance could bask in their greatness. So what we have here is this love, this mutual passion between the slow-witted Caius and quick-witted Yael; Caius is rich, Yael poor; Caius obtuse, Yael intelligent; Yael industrious, Caius lackadaisical. Caius seemed to expect that, because of his famous namesakes, the gods would raise him overnight to the rank of consul or praetor; he knew nothing about handling weapons and he was a lousy orator, but while Yael was tiny and slender, Caius was a giant of a figure, though his face was not so powerful as those of the other two Caiuses whom he carried so hopefully in his heart; however, his obtuseness was coupled with a certain kindliness and his face was girlishly hairless. To a hairy Jewish girl this could be very attractive. Though your name is Caius, the sharp-tongued Yael told him, you're beardless like Clodius, and your passion, like his, rises not at the prospect of power but at the sight of women; it's nothing to be sneezed at, though, it's also power! or, when you've had plenty of the fine wines of Hispania—poor Yael had no idea yet what the word Hispania meant coming from her mouth!—you seek your pleasure with pretty little boys, like my brother Caiaphas, whom, though I haven't seen him in a year, I love very much; yes, you do take more after Clodius; I'm thinking of the one, said the well-educated Yael, who dressed up as a girl and stole into the bedroom of Pompeia, Caesar's wife—he could get away with it for he was hairless—while the women were celebrating the holiday of Bona Dea, who, according to the Greeks, is none other than the mother of Dionysus; but don't pout so indecently, my dear Caius, said the clever Yael, because I love you anyway, yes, you, Caius, with the soul of Clodius and the body of Marius, I do, maybe because you are like that. The jewels of Jerusalem were no longer in fashion. Although sometimes she secretly did give herself to him, Yael could not belong to Caius. And some said that not only did the Jewess lie in the aristocratic bed but she had threatened Caius with a curse if she couldn't be his for good, which could happen only if he adopted the Jewish faith, an act he'd have to seal by drinking blood in a dark secret cellar, where her people, led by a certain Kristos, gathered on Saturdays to conspire and incite to rebellion. Under cover of night the large Jewish residences were set on fire and surrounded. Those who managed to escape the fire were run through with lances. That's how the uncle died, stabbed to death; and that's how his wife met her end, too, on the point of a lance; seven of their sons burned to death in the fire; Rufus and Rachel were drowned in the pool at the center of the atrium, where the pretty fountain bubbled; and the slaves weren't spared either, even though they had waited for neither a savior nor anything else. But somehow, no one knows how, Yael escaped. At dawn after that very same night a Jewish merchant set out for Hispania and took her along. She bore him ten children; she grew fat and became a very good mother. Six of her children were boys; together the six sons sired thirty-six sons. Thus she told her grandchildren what my grandfather told me. That is how the name that our ancestors bore dwindled slowly away, passing from son to son—Simon, Simeon. It would return later, when the family that had fallen apart was reunited in the converging blood. It wouldn't take long. But Yael could not have known that when she was telling stories to her grandchildren. The thirty-six boys carried Yael's blood to all parts of the world; through Yael they carried her own and Rufus's blood and, through Rufus, the blood of Simon, who had come from the tribe of Aaron. And another five hundred years went by, approximately. Times were hard. There lived a boy, a descendant of the grandsons, who became father to a girl, and because the father still remembered well, and because the baby girl was so beautiful even in the crib that people came to marvel at her, he named her Rachel in memory of the Rachel who was the first to come to Rome and thus, in a way, may be considered a progenitress. This young man had no other children. And to make sure his little girl was not taken from him, he took on the Christian faith, but he could not keep down the flesh of pork. He had to vomit it out. In his distress he sent a letter to Sura asking for the advice of the sages as to what Jews should do in their desperate straits, how they might keep the commands of their faith in the face of persecution. The reply took ten years to arrive. It came not in the form of a letter but in that of a merchant who wasn't really a merchant but a famous Gaon, and his name was Samuel ben Josef. In the meantime, Rachel had grown into a beautiful girl, and of course Samuel, who was given lodging in the house of the letter-writer, immediately fell in love with her. And this is how Samuel spoke to the assembled Jews: Remember! Enoch and his cohorts fell into the sin of idolatry, for which the Lord withdrew into the third heaven. And what do we call idolatry? If men, themselves creatures of the Lord, worship not the Lord but certain of His creatures. Living or dead. It is as if the Lord had fulfilled the promise of the curse and taken you among a people that neither you nor your fathers had known before, and where, as it is written, you will serve strange gods, even trees and stones. And what about dissembling? To dissemble is to lie, and it is also a sin, the Mishnah tells us. Therefore you are committing a double sin, and there is nothing I can do except to reprimand you most severely, and to pray for you. And now, until the sheep return to the fold, I shall stay here. And so he did. Rachel gave him twelve children. But thirty years later Samuel set out again to return to the Academy of Sura, where he had been a famous teacher before he left. They took the little ones with them. His two oldest sons, well-respected rabbis, stayed on in Cordova. But no news ever came from Sura or anywhere else, and the traces of Rachel, Samuel, and the little ones were lost forever. Maybe one day we'll discover them and they'll come back. Whenever someone knocks on your door, don't be surprised, you never can tell. Don't be surprised if in your dreams you speak in unfamiliar languages—Aramaic, Hebrew, Greek, Arabic, Latin, and, because of later times, many other tongues. It may be only a dream, but everything is true and everything is probable. So don't be amazed!"

A strange thud from the bathroom. The fish is out of the sink, thrashing about on the stone floor. Hurling itself up and up under the sink. Grandmama is pressing her hand to her face and her tears are dribbling out between her fingers. I am standing on a chair. The one Grandpapa had sat on. I have to laugh, because I can see myself peeing into the sink, but at the same time I'm grabbing the toothbrush and the pee is running through the toothbrush. And the fish is flopping around in the sink, where it would like to swim but has no room. Squelch. Squish. He is standing in the tub, soaping himself, he is lathering soap on his hair, I can hear the sounds of the soap and I can feel somebody watching me. Can I turn around? The woman with the glasses is watching me, and next to her, on the same chair I was just standing on, Uncle Frigyes is sitting. He's laughing. He jumps up and runs out, vanishes in the dark. I can feel that it's me in there, in the dark, it's me he's hugging, and now he forces the toothbrush into my mouth, breaking a tooth. Maybe I'm bleeding? Uncle Frigyes is laughing. I *am* bleeding, I'll bleed to death, it will all flow out. I am lying down somewhere. The stone is cold. I've no idea how I got here. A whole lot of things are happening, but I can't even move, all I can do is watch. Dark. Somebody is yelling, "If you cut your finger with a knife it would hurt, wouldn't it? Answer me!" "Yes, it would!" How interesting: it was my voice that answered but I can see my face, and the face didn't open its mouth. "That's how I'd cut into you, just as that knife did!" Maybe it was Grandpapa who shouted, "Yes, it will hurt!" Now I know where I am. The biggest pot is on the stove. The frying onion is turning black. So it was just now, after all, that I slid down the railing and fell all the way down here. But I'm waiting in vain, she cannot come, Grandmama is lying in her room, and if my blood keeps flowing like this I will die, too. So, it must have been now that I cut my finger. But this white leg is not of a person. A bed. Seems to be in our kitchen. They brought the beds from there. In the bathroom, too, the floor tiles are black and white. Where the fish still is. But at the windows curtains are billowing in the wind, the sun is shining into the room, the bloodstains are fluttering in the wind. Ten white ones. Double bunks, white walls. Nobody around. With nobody absent there would be twenty boys living here; there's always one of us in the sickroom. Must step only on the black tiles! Must wait. Somebody will come and then I'll leave, too. Strolling among the beds, stepping only on black tiles, never on white ones! But then I must not be here, after all, because this woman hadn't appeared yet, and I don't know why she's here; and if she's leaning over me, then I must be lying down. Lying somewhere. Her mouth is moving. Over black-and-white squares. It feels as if I'm lying right in the middle of something soft and white, but still on the cold stone, and this woman seems to be saying something; I can see her mouth move but I can't hear anything. Grandmama, she's the one who brings the chamber pot because I have to pee. Still, it's Grandpapa who is lying in the bed, not I. But how did the beds get there? Who did this? That's the way he always lay. Doesn't notice the fly landing on his eye. Has to be shooed away! He keeps looking because his eyes can't be shut. Grandmama covers the mirror, too, with a black kerchief. I don't know where the flies are coming from. Grandmama is waving a black kerchief, pulls the shutters to, closes the window, still the flies keep coming. I've got to chase them away. Candle sputters in the dark. She lit a candle over Grandpapa's head. Careful as we are, the floor still creaks when we walk. Then I'm here, after all? "I'm going now, to church, you stay with him, till the angel comes. The angel will come for him, don't worry!" She disappears. Wind is blowing outside, I can hear it, but just a while ago the sun was shining. Uncle Frigyes is coming down the road, stops. Grandpapa is running toward him. The sky is dark. Uncle Frigyes lifts a rose to his nose, smells it, and resumes walking. Grandpapa stops. The door flies open and from the doorway Grandmama calls out, "Welcome, Frigyes! Would you like matzoh or challah with your coffee?" But the two men hug each other and Grandpapa is crying. Uncle Frigyes asks, "Your stool?" "It's all right now. Taking craps in the cellar." Grandmama serves challah with the coffee. Fat raisins in the white challah. The light blue eyes of Uncle Frigyes. "Why are you crying? If you are here, my dear, if I can feel your weight in my arms, that means we're alive! We're still alive, my dear!" Grandpapa lowers his head onto Uncle Frigyes's shoulder. "That's just it!" The swishing flight of white tablecloth. "This is the finest damask. Still from the trousseau of Grandpapa's mother, may she rest in peace. Be careful with it! I've only used it twice before! Don't make a mess on it!" Three cups on the table, the third one is for me. Viennese porcelain. Maria Theresa was the ruler back then. Silver spoons and that crystal platter for the whipped cream, let's put those out, too! Sliced challah in a small silver basket. Two hands on the damask tablecloth, among the cups and silverware. "What do you mean, That's just it!?" Grandpapa's bony hand is kneading Uncle Frigyes's cushioned hand. "That's just it! When you come to visit it's as if something had returned from the past, something that shouldn't, it fools me, something that's not what it used to be, something that's not alive any more because it's dead inside me. But it comes back, it's moving about, showing me its new pictures, even though my past has already turned to stone; for me, even you are already dead! I loved you! and I'd like to ask all of you, Don't disturb my stones! and if you never came to see me it would be as if I'd died, too, only I didn't notice when. What is still happening to me is so little, it's not life any more, more like the little events of death! Don't you feel that?" Uncle Frigyes's cushioned hand now kneads Grandpapa's bony hand on the table. He laughs. "You're showing your colors! And I can see through you! You little fool. You with your moaning and groaning. Sentimental Jew!" The candle, smoking and sputtering above Grandpapa's head, pearls running down the side of the candle. A fly is buzzing, crawling down his nose toward the big hole; it will crawl in! It's as if I were lying in his place, though I'm sitting here, but it's not him! something is lying there, something that resembles me or *is* me. I should do something! Jump up! But something holds me down. I can't make a move. I'm sitting here, or lying there, because the whole thing could be some mistake, and I failed to notice that in the meantime a son was born to me, and a grandson, and I've grown old and died and now that boy who is me is looking at me. Or maybe I've just gotten sleepy, Grandmama told me to stay here, and I've been dreaming and now I'm waking up? Where could I go? But Grandpapa is sitting in his armchair, his hand on the maroon velvet. But that's not Grandpapa's hand, it's mine! But Grandpapa suddenly snatches his hand away, a cup is tipped over, and in his fury his neck and mouth turn black. "You can't say that! You should have understood by now that I'm myself, me, *me*, ME!" But Uncle Frigyes closes his eyes and wheezes. "I only said it to get your goat, because when you're furious you can feel that you're alive!" Grandpapa is not laughing. "This is serious. Go ahead, laugh! And don't try to hide your laughter, either, it's as sharp as a knife! That's exactly how you tell me—with that suppressed laughter, you knife!—that all my ideas, my whole life has been one big mistake!" A gray shadow scoots behind the beam. The shadows are rejoicing. A whimpering voice: Grandpapa, let's have a story! Grandpapa, I can't remember anything! I can hear it, this whimpering voice inside me, and Grandmama was still not coming and then maybe I was just dreaming, after all. The shape of the body showed very distinctly under the cover, and the clasped hands sank into the softness of the blue silk; weight; flies on the wall and on his forehead and around his nose. The flame of the candle, its tiny crackling noises. Outside, the sounds of the wind, the light filtering in through the slats of the shutters, and the little rumblings of my stomach. I didn't get breakfast. It's something Grandmama forgot today. Once I ate all the whipped cream, while the two of them were fighting, but I threw up that evening. Uncle Frigyes always dropped lots of crumbs on the carpet. He broke the challah into crumbs and gesticulated with a piece in his hand. "Serious, you say? I don't know, my dear, if there is anything in the world we humans can talk about seriously. I prefer to laugh. At you. I'm laughing at you, too! Mistake? You mean an error, deviating from the truth? But what truth? Your whole life a mistake? Your ideas? Ideas can be directed only toward some goal. But who knows what the goals are? Maybe God? You've called it a mistake, my dear, not me. Ideas and mistakes, goals and truth, these are the two couples of the quadrille. Dancing gracefully. If you like your own ideas, then let doubt be yours, too. I have no doubts, because I have no ideas either, and I have no ideas because I see no goals, and since there are no goals, I don't know, I know nothing, so I've entrusted myself to God. Are you familiar with the Portuguese story?" "I am!" "I'm thinking about Simon Maimi, who died, walled up in a dungeon, but did not convert to Christianity though the other Jews did!" "I know the story, that Simon is a distant relative of mine! But how dare you preach to me? And what are you talking about, anyway? Did I set the fire under the stake? I did take off my clothes, but I never shed my faith! That's only a secular pretense! I got as far as my own soul. My own! All the way to my soul that turns only to God! And this soul, private, and my own, cannot be ranked with any herd or flock!" "Be quiet! Let me continue!" "Don't bother, I know the story very well!" "The end, you don't know the end of it!" "The end of what? It has no end!" Grandpapa yelled. Uncle Frigyes was also shouting. And they wouldn't let go, kept pulling and squeezing each other's hands among the cups and utensils on the table. Uncle Frigyes dunked the challah into the coffee, and when it soaked up the coffee he ate it. Grandpapa's denture was in a mug next to the candle. Grandmama said we'd put it away because everything that's left of Grandpapa is a memento. Uncle Frigyes would also roll little balls out of the challah and bombard Grandpapa with them. They were laughing and Grandmama said she wouldn't come and sit with them because she couldn't stand the way they were behaving. Like idiots. "*Ruhe!* You can't possibly know the end! Last spring, the Jews in Oporto, who had converted five hundred years ago built a synagogue to the God of the Jews and returned to the Jewish faith!" Uncle Frigyes yelled. Grandpapa yelled back, "And in another five hundred years, what will happen five hundred years from now, do you know? Five hundred years! There is no such thing as time! that's the mistake, there is no time! only me, me! Only I exist, the one actually present! Me!" Uncle Frigyes looked at Grandpapa, let go of his hand, wiped his forehead, and wheezed. "What about Job and that long debate about him, you know about Job?" Grandpapa laid his upturned palm on the white tablecloth and Uncle Frigyes put his hand into it. "Job? I get it. You knife, you!" And Grandpapa leaned over the table and kissed Uncle Frigyes's hand. And then they just sat there and cried. Grandpapa was moaning, Uncle Frigyes was sniveling but wanted to laugh. "You, my dear, no matter how much you protest, you are a chosen one. You have chosen yourself. You, yourself, with your own mind. By yourself. While I blended into what was given me by other minds. And I wrapped myself in the garb you shed. My dear! Here I sit, buttoned to the top, and you, stripped to the skin, are sitting here with me. That's how the two of us are, sitting on top of the world. Two old fools! And in the end just two ideas, only ideas, which are nothing but ignorance. And in the end we are brothers in ignorance." Uncle Frigyes was as tall as Grandpapa, but he was fat. When Grandpapa died Uncle Frigyes couldn't come over because he wasn't alive either, but Grandmama said she didn't want to tell me about it before. I don't know what happened to his watch. He probably died while we were eating the fish and the phone rang. On Friday. Fat people had to have special coffins made for them, Grandmama said. On his large belly an additional little bulge. That was the watch in his vest pocket. That watch struck every half hour, playing a little tune. As if his belly were making music. When he came and settled in the armchair, he'd draw me between his legs and I had to put my head to his belly; then he'd detach the watch chain from the button of his vest and hand me the watch. While they talked I lay in bed and waited for the watch to make music. When it struck I closed my eyes and the tune followed in the dark, but my joy was short-lived, for the tune was quickly over and then I had to wait again. We finished the coffee and the two of them were holding each other's hands. It was Grandpapa telling a story now. "I don't know if I've ever told you that on the way home I came through Cracow. In front of a house there was a huge crowd. I stopped, too, to see what they were gaping at. A bomb had created a perfect cross section of that house, so that in the intact halves of the rooms you could see pictures hanging on the wall and pillows scattered on the sofas, all a little dusty; on the third floor, I don't know why, a chamber pot was right in the middle of a table with a singed lace tablecloth; on the fourth floor in a room with silk drapes there stood an upright piano against the wall. In the split staircase a man was going up, that's what the crowd was watching, and I directed my attention to him, too. He was an older man; he stopped at every floor, rested, then moved on. On the fourth floor he put his key in the lock, opened the door, then shut it behind him. In the hallway he hung his coat on the coatrack. Went into the room. Looked around, smiled, drew his finger across a chair, noticed how dusty it was; then he sat down at the piano and opened the lid. He looked at the keyboard for a long time, sunk in thought. Those of us down on the street were standing and watching in complete silence. I think the Poles knew who he was. And then he began to play, I think something by Chopin. But he was playing for himself, practicing, getting his hands used to the instrument. When he missed a note he'd start over again from the beginning, and that allowed the same melody to show its many different sides. This made the whole thing more beautiful. The crowd was growing, really swelling. Many people cried. The strange performance lasted for more than an hour. Then the man got up, stretched his back and pelvis, and started for a door, which opened into air. And he yanked the door with him, frame and all, and the frame yanked with it the whole remaining section of the wall." The watch struck and played its little tune. Uncle Frigyes got up and asked, "You made up this story, didn't you? Didn't you? you made it up, answer me!" Grandpapa didn't answer. Uncle Frigyes laughed. "You did, I know! Life isn't like that, I know! You made it up, didn't you? I know it!" Uncle Frigyes laughed, plopped back down into the armchair so hard that a chair leg broke. He sat on the floor and kept laughing. When he left we pushed the chair out of the room and under the stairs in the hallway, to be repaired later. That night there was a knock on the window. The silk shoes I stole out of the closet were near my bed. I had to hide them somewhere quickly. "Open up, it's me!" In the window a head wearing an army cap: my father. I won't turn on the light, and then I can be alone with him, Grandmama won't know about it! I couldn't find the silk shoes and knocked over a chair. I reached forward. He was stamping his feet impatiently at the door. I couldn't find the key because it was in the lock. The key must be kept in the lock, that way thieves can't put in their picklock. My father's face was stubbly and warm. His clothes had that smell. If Grandmama doesn't wake up I'll find the benzene and clean his clothes. "Father, I'll clean your clothes! I'll find the benzene and wash them for you!" In the bathroom we turned on the light, but I had to cover my eyes and I couldn't see him. The fish was asleep at the bottom of the tub, but the light woke it up. "Grandmama managed to get fish!" "No need to clean them, because I must leave early in the morning!" He gave me his clothes, and there he was standing naked, and I liked to see him naked. Grandpapa said that according to the Torah nobody should see the nakedness of his father. Éva said that nakedness meant the prick. "Could I sleep with you then, Father?" "I almost forgot, I've brought you something. Give me my pants! And run some water in the sink. We'll put the fish there for the meanwhile." While he was looking in his pants pockets for what he'd brought me, I filled the sink with water, but didn't look back, just waited to see what the present might be. It was something like the cartridge Csider once gave me, only empty. "It's a whistle. Blow it!" In the sink, the fish was flopping about, wanting to swim but didn't have enough room. In the shower my father was standing with his eyes closed. I sat on the chair and occasionally blew the whistle so he could see I was glad to have it. I was so excited to be sitting there, because there he was soaping himself and tonight I could sleep in the same bed with him. And then the door opened a crack and I saw Grandmama blinking in the light and shouting, "Feri! Feri! And you, what are you blowing that whistle for in the middle of the night?" But instead of coming in she ran back out. The whistle vanished. At night there was no kerchief or hat on Grandmama's head, and when she brought the chamber pot and I yelled, She's bringing the potty! bringing the potty! what I really wanted to yell was, Here comes Baldy! here comes Baldy!—but I never did. Grandmama came back, running, with a kerchief on her head. "You want me to scrub your back? Kneel down, son, I'll scrub it for you." He knelt down in the tub and Grandmama began soaping his back. She was talking in rhythm with her work. "Should I clean your clothes? I'll do it quickly, in benzene! Are you hungry? What shall I give you? Will eggs be all right?" We could hear Grandpapa calling from far away, and then he opened the door wide, but stopped there. "I've been waiting for you! Trouble! Big trouble! *Die letzte Woche wurde Frigyes Sohn verhaftet!*"* Father slipped out from under Grandmama's hands and stood up. "Aren't you going to wash your hair? Should I wash it for you, son?" "What do you want me to do, Father?" "You're asking me? He's your friend!" Father got under the shower and closed his eyes. The water was rushing over his glistening body and gurgling into the drain under his feet. "Youthful nonsense! If he was arrested, he probably gave them a good reason for it." Grandpapa was shouting. *"Er war doch dein Freund!"*† Father opened his eyes and whispered, and Grandpapa leaned for-

* "Frigyes's son was arrested last week."
† "He was your friend, though."

ward to read the words on his lips. "Friendships also pass, Father, when a stable world finally takes shape. Unfortunately, I'm more and more set in my ways." "But we're not talking about you. Can it be that you're not bound by any morals or the times we live in?" "Papa! Stop shouting! Can't you see he's just got home? Son! Eggs, then?" "What first has to be made clear, Father, is where one stands. Then come morals. Towel, please!" Grandmama didn't know where to rinse off her soapy hands and using only two fingers she opened the closet and pulled out a towel. "Parties! For me there's been only one party, always. Go on, laugh, you know how that offends me! But ever since God created the world man has always had two parties, Cain's and Abel's! But of course you're right, I can only side with one!" "Let's not argue, Father, I'm tired." "The hunter and the hunted!" "Here, son, the towel!" "Papa, I can't find my whistle!" "And if you ask me where I stand, I can answer only that I stand here. I'm here, in the bathroom. I'm the hunted, not the hunter." "The towel, son!" Father laughed and stepped out of the tub and took the towel. The whistle must have rolled under the tub. "I'm sorry, Father, but this is all so moving and beautiful that I have to throw up!" The fish was thrashing in the sink. Father was drying himself. The water hadn't been turned off and was pouring out of the showerhead, and the drain was sucking it away loudly. Father led the way out, with the towel around his waist. Grandmama ran behind him. Grandpapa made a big effort to keep up, too. From here, from the bathroom, I saw the room I'm so rarely allowed to enter. When Grandmama was cleaning it I'd go in with her, or in the afternoon when everybody was napping. The nicest room in the house. There is no carpet, with every step the floor creaks, and the whitewashed walls are completely blank. No curtains at the window, no need for them because the sun doesn't come in here; outside, three enormous pine trees, and the dark shadows of the pines move on the walls inside the room. Here I can be relaxed; nobody can slip behind my back. On the big bed a soft green blanket. Just to be lying there and imagining that he is there next to me. In front of the window a long table on nice bentwood legs, and the cushions of the armchair covered with the same soft green as the bedcover. The tabletop is clean, empty; there is only one drawer, but it's always locked, because that's where the most important papers are kept. That's where I stole the Nina Potapova textbook from, on a Sunday morning. Csider can search in the attic all he wants; everything that's secret is here, but I can't tell anyone that. And there's nothing else in the room. Still, when we light the chandelier the whole place glows, nice and not too brightly. Again Grandpapa said something and stopped in the middle of the room, under the light of the chandelier. Father tore the towel off his waist.

How large, how hairy, how naked! The soft green bedcover had the same smell as when I dug my head into his shoulder; in the middle of the cover a stain or a worn spot, I couldn't tell. Grandmama hands him clean pajamas. Each time he leaves, Grandmama washes and irons so he'll have clean linen no matter when he might return. When he's gone, Grandmama and I keep waiting for his letter or telegram. But the mailman doesn't come in, only calls out from the gate, because he's afraid of the dog. But my dog doesn't bite. When it shows its teeth, that's a smile, but everybody thinks he's going to bite them. Once, one Sunday morning, Grandmama couldn't take me to Mass because Father had come home on Saturday. The sun shone into the hallway, where he was looking at himself in the mirror. "I'm getting gray. Take out the hammer and some nails; we're going to make a letterbox. Out of what? I don't know yet." We looked for something under the stairs, among broken things and suitcases. He found an old drawer. We made the letterbox out of that. It turned out like a little house, with a door and a window and a slanting roof so the rain would run off it. And then the mailman didn't shout anymore, just threw the mail in the letterbox. When the dog died, it showed its teeth. I would have liked to close its mouth, but I couldn't. The mailman still wouldn't come to the house. It was no use standing by the window all morning waiting for a letter or telegram. It always came unexpectedly. The small room with all the closets and the sewing things was dark and hot. I was running toward the room that was light, because suddenly I wanted to see his eyes. "How should I talk, dear God? As in prayer, I would like to ask that You put the words into my mouth!" When he let me lie next to him and he hadn't turned the light off, I'd always look at his eyes, because I couldn't understand what made them so blue, what could that be? "Oh, son, please put on your pajamas, you'll catch cold!" Then, that Sunday morning, I snuggled next to him in bed. He was lying there naked. I would have liked to take off my pajamas, too, but was scared to, I don't know why. That way I could have felt him more. I dug my head into his shoulder, I could smell the cover, and I pressed my body on his. But he quickly pushed me away. "Get out of here! Go! Get back to your bed, go on! Get out of here! Go!" He took the pajama pants from Grandmama and tossed the wet towel into the armchair, but it fell on the floor. "Cat got your tongue?" "Again? Are we starting again, Father?" "I'm terribly frightened! I know what's awaiting you!" Father unfolded the neatly ironed pajama pants and, as if trying them for size, covered his lower body with them; he thought for a long time, burst out laughing, then waved the empty pants before Grandpapa. "Come on, Father! I'm sorry, I just can't help laughing. What do you know,

Father? Really, where do you stand? I don't think you stand, or even exist anywhere any more!" "I'm still alive! In case you haven't noticed, I'm telling you I'm still alive! And as long as one is alive, the words that are said, the thoughts that are expressed, spread, have an influence, even if one can't do anything, and you can't stop that! Don't you see? You can wash all you want! You're covered in blood! What will you do before God's judgment? Son?" "Don't talk to me about God!" "How could God let such a devil issue from me?" "Enough! I'm fed up!" "Fed up?" "With your biblical curses, yes, fed up!" "So you're fed up? Is it my turn to laugh now? Hahaha! In fact, you're frightened. Frightened of the abyss my words have opened at your feet! Fear and trembling! Fear that if your past won't vindicate you—and I am the past, your past, too!—then you are still bloody and will plunge into the depths, into the abyss, which I make you see and open before you!" "Enough! Do you hear me? Enough!" "Son! Papa! Son! The eggs?" "If I didn't have to take into consideration who you are, sir! you, with whom I've never had anything in common, not even for a moment—yes, it's true, I've wheedled money out of you, but luckily never for myself, and only because I knew it would do some good, and because that was the only useful thing about you ever, your money, which you've given me so that now I can choke you with it; don't you understand? we don't reciprocate! what you got in return was that you could happily admire yourself! because with selflessness you don't have even a nodding acquaintance, your every act is hypocrisy and a lie, you've always protected your virginity because you're a coward, always have been! I hate your impossible flowery rhetoric, your filthy desires sublimated into spirituality! You've never lived, haven't you noticed? You have never lived! Yes, you've been around, but you've never lived! If I didn't take into consideration that unfortunately you're my father, then right now, as befits a murderer, I'd slap you good and hard and make sure your shitty thoughts spread no further, not even to *my* ears!" "Hideous! My God, could I be that guilty, am I that guilty? Will I be arrested by my own son? Here, here I am." "Get your hands away! Don't be a martyr! Not for me, not even that! You make me sick! Do you understand? I'll tear you to pieces as I'm tearing up this rag. Get the hell out of my room, you hear?" I was holding on to the door. Grandpapa spread his arms. Father ripped his pajamas in two. A strange thud from the bathroom. The fish was out of the sink, thrashing about on the floor. I was holding the fish, but it was slippery, it wouldn't let me help. I pressed it against me, and put it back into the tub, ran the water for it. Grandmama was crying and ran into the kitchen. My pajamas were slimy. Father slammed and locked all the connecting doors, locking himself in his room. When the tub was filled up, the fish began to swim. It was quiet. This is where Grandpapa told me the story of the fish-smelling girl. It was when Grandmama had gone to the market that up in the attic Grandpapa told me the stories about our ancestors, the day Grandmama brought home the fish. "I'm telling it to you as my grandfather told me in Szernye, on the bench under the mulberry tree." Grandpapa was sitting on the chair I had sat on when Father was soaping himself and the fish was flopping around in the sink. But now he was whispering: "Don't look at me! I don't exist any more!" I was looking at the black-and-white tile floor. The skylight was made of wired glass. I couldn't imagine how they had got the netting into the glass. I kept looking at it. That's where the light was plummeting down, slanted, into the attic. Now! Now! Now it's rushing down! It would be great to see the instant when the light began, or when it ended. "Don't look! Just listen! The story has no end, it will continue in you, and you may pass it on. If you can. Let me go on, then, still as my grandfather told it to me. I almost said to myself, Watch what you're saying! watch your mouth! when you say that the two oldest sons of Samuel ben Josef stayed in Cordova. Is that what I was saying?" "Yes!" "That's how I answered back then, too, but this is how my grandfather from Szernye continued: Then I made a mistake, for while they planned it that way, that's not what happened, and I don't want to lie. The plans and wishes of the participants are of minor importance in this story. We have to stick to the facts. And the facts in the exquisite mechanism of this story mesh like fine gears: one spurring on the next; the tiniest grain of a lie is enough to make them squeak and the whole thing grinds to a halt! Oh no! Not so with history! The meshing of history's gears is mysteriously perfect; no grain of dust can get into them because the mechanism is covered with a bell jar, like a cheese in a fine store. But our narrative will be called careless if we are not cautious enough. And in this case caution means sticking to the facts. *Zu den Tatsachen*. Therefore, I correct myself: the family set out on donkeys and traveled across the valley of the Guadalquivir. All the way down to the sea.

"In Cádiz they sold their surplus donkeys, keeping only two: Reuben's, a plain gray ass, and Judah's, which was no plain donkey: it was all white. The two boys stood on the shore. When a favorable breeze took the ship over the horizon, they were ready to start back, but under Judah's weight the pretty white donkey kept collapsing. Reuben checked the animal: This breaks my heart! I think it's the burden of separation that the donkey can't carry. Thus Judah moaned and wailed. You're crazy! Thus Reuben, known for his pragmatism. This donkey is sick. We'll sell it. We might even get some small change for its hide. We'll add to that and buy another one. Judah, who was more sensitive than clever, argued, How can we sell its hide while it's still alive? How? And if I'm crazy, then just go on by yourself! I'm going to a doctor! Reuben burst out laughing. Why would you do that? Who's sick, you or the donkey? By now Judah was shouting, I'm taking the donkey! Reuben continued with his teasing: Yourself? Donkey to the doctor? The doctor's no jackass! Judah took off at a run, tugging and pulling the sick donkey after him and yelling, Go ahead, go on by yourself! I'll manage! I'm not going with you! Reuben got on his donkey and trotted off in the opposite direction, but not before shouting back, You're as dull as your donkey! King of Donkeys! That's how Reuben returned to Cordova. And that's why Judah stayed in Cádiz, because of the sick donkey. A little boy showed him the way. They strolled across town—the boy in front, followed by the donkey, Judah ogling at everything, trudging behind them. They had gone past all the houses when the little boy stopped. There! That one! That's the house! A path led to it, bordered with olive trees and bountiful wildflowers. When the bearded old man standing in front of the house learned that the donkey's owner was the son of Samuel ben Josef, he bowed and said nothing for a long time. I don't know, he said finally, I only hope I have enough knowledge to cure the donkey. I am acquainted with, and greatly respect, the erudition of your father. His wisdom searches the infinite. As for me, I seek simple solutions for the finite flesh. I shall do my best. But if my eyes don't deceive me, in things spiritual you are not your father's inferior, and I would be delighted if you would honor my house with your presence while your donkey is ailing. The old man's daughter, a pale-faced beauty, washed Judah's feet. And that house! Judah had never seen anything like it! Filled with animals! Each after its kind, just as Noah had received them into and then released them from his ark. I can't tell you how many there were! In one room monkeys were chasing one another; a large wildcat was lounging in a corner. Above them, red, yellow, and blue birds were swinging and screeching on long rods, and all the birds of the forest were flying round and round: woodpecker, titmouse, thrush, magpie, owl, and tree sparrow, countless birds! wrynecks and collared flycatchers, and in one cage there were thirty turtledoves and thirty pigeons; and woodchats and warblers and siskins and sparrow hawks and all kinds of finches. In the second room, in separate quarters, lived the crocodile and the cobra; the latter was coiled up nicely, napping while a hedgehog licked its head; there were also green-bellied lizards and hard-backed stag beetles, flies, bedbugs, fleas, lice, and innumerable centipedes. In the third room lived the dogs, big and small, along with six deer and seven fawns, and three antelopes, and a weasel running around at their hooves; also a few tuft-tailed polecats and lots of squirrels. And in the fourth room, fish were swimming in a pool: the stingray, this frightening black pancake, and pretty starfish, and carp, sea bream, perch, trout, bullhead, and gudgeon, and squid with a hundred tentacles, and soft jellyfish—a very pleasant company, I must say!—and at poolside a stork couple, wild ducks, herons, and white seagulls. Judah was amazed. As if this were the place he had been looking for all along. As if in my dream, my days were spent in marvels and miracles, truly, and I felt at ease because the donkey got better and gradually regained its strength. And in the fifth room, in the midst of the wild noise and infernal stench of the animals, in front of the window, sat the pale-faced girl. With golden thread she embroidered fine silks with patterns of plants, nothing but plants. And I learned much from the old man, too. I learned that there's poison in the fangs of the cobra, and it can be used to cure leprosy; and the liver of hedgehogs, mixed well with isinglass and pulverized, is an excellent remedy for donkey ailments. And he also taught me that parrot droppings relieve toothaches, and the venomous secretion of flatfish, smeared on a cow's rear end, can ease her calving pains. Disorder? shouted the old man in the animal cacophony, this is God's order! Judah also liked to sit next to the pale-faced girl. The girl looked up: You've asked me, Judah, why I keep at this embroidery day after day. I don't know myself, since those who wear it die, every one of them, and the silk and the gold stitches decay along with their bodies. I think I should embroider the wind, that's what I think, and then everyone could see my patterns, see the many tendrils, buds, and flowers of my soul glowing and fluttering gently about us in the air, against the great blue sky. Yes, that's how beautifully she spoke. Judah asked her to be his wife, and from her he learned all about plants. Later our old father died and the two of us were left there among the animals. And they all lived happily together. In a big book Judah noted down everything he experienced, the things he already knew and even those he hadn't yet learned, all the great life questions that remained. He hardly noticed that in the meantime four daughters were born to him, because the animals were also multiplying in great numbers. As though in passing, the owner of a sick bull told them that Tarik's hordes had crossed the sea and might pose great danger. And one night Cádiz was set on fire. The animals bellowed, moaned, squawked, and screeched. Only the crocodile stayed calm, though lazily it opened an eye. The flames of the burning city illuminated the inside of the house and Judah's daughters wept, even though here, among the animals, they were never afraid of anything. Only the shadows of the animals on the wall, that's what we were so frightened of! The wildcat jumped up on the roof and growled. And then a sooty shadow of a figure stopped by our house and shouted inside, Whether you stay or run away, make sure you keep to yourselves, keep apart! Don't get the rest of the poor Jews into trouble! But why? our father called back, surprised. Wasn't it you who gave the Visigoths' secret battle plans to Tarik? the breathless stranger managed to say before taking off. But our mother was very calm as she went from room to room. First she opened the cage of the turtledoves and pigeons and said, Go on, fly! Then came all the birds of the meadow and forest. She released the monkeys, and the monkeys somersaulted away into the red night. The serpent slid under the door and silently vanished. The antelope ran to the north, the grasshoppers popped off in all directions, the insects crawled about briskly or took to the air if they had wings. Only the crocodile showed some reluctance, but your grandmother kept poking at it until it finally dragged itself outside, looked around, oriented itself, and set out for the Nile delta. When only the ever-silent fish were left, Great-grandmother looked at Great-grandfather. We're ready! And they loaded up the white donkey and the family took to the road. To Uncle Reuben in Cordova. Of course one should know that when it's night in Cádiz, it's already dawn in Baghdad. And who would have known that the tramp Shaprut would decide to leave Baghdad that dawn, his destination unclear even to himself. Shaprut is a young man with all his possessions on his back. Shaprut cannot sleep in the same bed two nights in a row. Always on the road, his eyes burning with an inner fire, his eyelids, irritated by sand and light, always red and bleary. Where are you coming from, Shaprut, and where to now? I don't know. Blindly ahead. Following my nose. I think that's the safest direction! But no matter how many miles Shaprut would cover, the earth is round—of course Shaprut couldn't have known that—and just by walking he could never leave himself behind, and that's why there was no place where he would find what he was looking for. Six years later he wound up in Cordova. There he asked not only for lodging but also for the hand of Judah's oldest daughter. Could this be what he had been looking for? The young couple slept together for two nights in a row, and for two days in a row Shaprut told stories. One day I'll tell you Shaprut's stories. And then he disappeared again. He left not a single trace behind, only a germinating seed. When this seed sprouts, six months from now, we shall be entering the second circle. Because the story has seven circles. My grandfather told me about six, and the seventh is ours. The first, Rufus's, was the circle of beauty, and that had come to an end, and the end was failure: beauty faded away completely in Shaprut's wondrous tales. The second circle, the one coming up now, is the circle of reason, and in this one, in the heady daze of tales, our progenitor Hasdai ibn Shaprut was conceived. Look, the gate now stands open! That's what Hasdai said when he was telling stories to his grandson. Because he believed that reason would surely open the way to happiness, because he didn't know what my grandfather didn't know either, what only I know: that behind the gates opening out one to the other, there are closed walls, and the circle doesn't break anywhere and always returns to itself. But I'm going on with the story, just as my grandfather did. He said something important about Hasdai's birth. Hasdai's mother was only in her seventh month when he was born, but he survived. He had seven teeth, seven hairs on his head, and his head was so large that his mother died in giving him birth. At seven years of age, Hasdai spoke seven living languages. By the time he was fourteen, Hasdai wrote poetry in seven languages. 'Rose' is the name of the poem that our forebears passed on by word of mouth from generation to generation, and now it reaches you, too. This is how it goes:

its proud regal red
is not red enough for it
its spilled redness—blood

"I hope you appreciate the poem's crudely beautiful music. I believe he used this fine allusion to speak of his own mortal anguish. His favorite book was the one his grandfather had written about animals. And he was only a beardless twenty-one when Christians, Jews, Visigoths, and Arabs were already seeking him out with their various ailments. He had a notable reputation. That is what got him to the court of the caliph. Listen! I'm telling you: court physician at the age of twenty-one, three times seven! The number seven! The mystery of seven makes its appearance in the second circle! Just as there are seven lands and seven heavens, to those in the realm of the second circle everything will happen under the sign of the number seven. But you have to know that at that time there lived a handsome king named Sancho. This king was a sworn enemy of the caliph. Whenever Sancho met someone he would show off his abdominals, his calves, his biceps: Look, miserable worm, I'm made of the same stuff as you, yet how perfect I am! Not a gram of fat under my skin! Then, from one day to the next, the valiant king, so enamored with himself, began to put on weight. At first he weighed about a hundred kilograms, like a prize hog. Despite the efforts of many famous doctors, by the second day the king doubled in size, and on the seventh day he weighed close to a ton. Messengers carried the word everywhere: anyone who can cure the king may ask for anything in return, that's the message of the bloated king. Before getting to work, this is how Hasdai addressed the king: I'm not asking for money, land, gold, a castle, or wealth. My only wish is that if I have the good fortune to cure you, you will come with me to Cordova and make amends with the caliph, whom you consider to be your archenemy and who is my benevolent master. Of course the ballooning king agreed. And the miracle did happen. Though it was no miracle. Hasdai crushed the head of a serpent, tapped a small amount of blood from a lemur, and dried it on the bellies of green lizards, then added some pepper and other spices: the mixture was fed to a pigeon. The pigeon laid an egg. The king ate the egg. In two days he lost two hundred kilograms, and on the seventh day his abdomen was back to normal, and once again he twittered to his servants like this: See how beautiful I am? Am I not beautiful? And this silk waist cloth on my loins is so very becoming, is it not? And happily he went off to Cordova and made his peace with the caliph, which he did gladly, because he could put on airs and haughtily parade his self-declared beauty for the rest of his life. That's how Hasdai was both a great doctor and a peacemaker. Out of gratitude, the caliph made him a minister, so Hasdai became very rich as well. Therefore he may also be called wise. In his free time he interested himself in astronomy, poetry, and translation. Dioscorides' work on botany was given to him by the ambassador of Byzantium; first he translated it into Latin, then turned it into beautifully polished Arabic. Because at that time and place the Jews were Arabs. And he was a magnificent correspondent. It was due to his eloquence that the King of Khazar —ruler of an independent state north of the Black Sea—having read Hasdai's convincing arguments, converted to Judaism along with his entire nation. That's how the Khazars became Jews. And still, there was one great sorrow in Hasdai's life. He had no sons. And the oldest of his seven daughters became pregnant. But they couldn't find out—no! no! she wouldn't tell—who had gotten her with child. And she wouldn't tell, even after Hasdai had beaten her several times in succession. It was as if, in beating this miserable little hussy so mercilessly, Hasdai was taking out his anger at his own birth, his whole life; he was hissing while he beat her. And strangely, the girl did not object to the beating. But why would this bright jewel in the Star of David be angry at his own life? one might ask if one did not know Hasdai's heart. Hasdai's life was ruled by his mind. And the mind—Hasdai couldn't have known this, and neither could my grandfather—is not enough for life. Even when he embraced his wife, twice a week according to the Torah's permissive command, even then Hasdai could not entrust himself to his instincts, because his mind, to the rhythm of his instincts, prayed like this: Let it be a boy! let it be a boy! be a boy, my seed! God grant me my wish! The foolish sin of the mind is the will. And the girl whom he so enjoyed beating and who found pleasure in it, his daughter, was now saying this: What I've done, believe me, I didn't do out of lustfulness, no, Father! Even this beating is better than the pleasure I had! I am your daughter, I am yours! Oh, Father, I was urged on by some kind—I don't know what kind, but some high, highest kind—of reason, Father. I know it's hard to countenance; even your sagacity is inadequate for this, Father! Not even you can know the future! And now I'll be leaving! We thought that the girl had disappeared forever. In Malaga she gave birth to her child, who, for reasons we don't know, was given the name Samuel ibn Nagdela. The family thought the girl had killed herself. In his sorrow, Hasdai established an academy for higher learning in Cordova, the one where Moses ben Enoch spread the wisdom of rabbinical studies. But Samuel did come into the world and it was he—see, the girl was not lying!—who sent the family's fame soaring in intellectual and learned circles. His mind, like a crystal, cut through to all knowledge and also illuminated all knowledge. The mother, working as a lowly servant, did not reveal the secret of his birth to Samuel but sent him to study at her father's academy in Cordova. That's where Samuel and Hasdai met, and the old man was enraptured by the boy and loved him greatly; he didn't know it was his grandson. Yet he must have felt it, because it was to this boy he chose to tell his stories. Therefore, whenever God brings you together with a stranger, be careful! be polite, kind, calm, but also on guard, because you never know, the stranger might be of your own blood! And if in the end you open your heart, that may turn out to be your best investment. Samuel could read, write, and speak in seven languages. He could decipher secrets of the future by reading the stars. The rose, this curious family plant that opens its fiery velvet flowers atop rigid thorny stems, inspired him also, just as it had his grandfather, to compose a poem. And the poem has survived, I can quote it to you:

thou flower of enfeebled hearts
oh rose
set our fine silks aglow!

"You've got it? How much more pleasing its sounds than those of Hasdai's poem! Showy but lacking depth. Like Samuel's life. He is the one who strove highest in the circle of reason and intellect; therefore he's the one who had to fall. Suddenly one night Cordova was in flames, by morning it was reduced to ashes. Samuel sought refuge in Granada. His mother was still alive, surviving by working as a servant, stealing, and pinching pennies. She had time before her death to tell her son that the man he admired as his master was his grandfather; as to his father, well, that was of no importance, and she did not reveal his identity to Samuel: I needed him only to have you! With the money his dead mother left him, Samuel opened a small store, but at an excellent location! Sometimes, when I look around, I have the feeling that this is actually Samuel's little store, and I am Samuel, and what was to happen to him then could happen to me now. Here I am, sitting among spices and silks—not exactly local goods!—the gate across the street opens, and a servant comes over from the palace of King Habbus. When he returns to the palace, loaded down with goods, this is how he addresses King Habbus: Sire! Just opposite the palace lives a Jew who's at home in all the sciences, his mind is like the sharpest razor, he writes poetry, speaks reads and writes in seven languages. So the king sends for me and tells me to get rid of this wretched little excuse for a store; he's been looking for a capable secretary for a long time. And I go without a word. And my grandfather was laughing so hard he was plucking his beard. I didn't understand why he was laughing. Of course I quickly remember, said my grandfather, still choking with laughter, that it's not King Habbus who lives across the street but Grünfeld! But that's how Samuel's star rose. First he was only a secretary, but then a minister. He founded an academy, and for its library he managed to acquire the tomes of the Talmud from the Academy of Sura, the same volumes his great-grandfather, the famous

Samuel ben Josef, had used when he was teaching there before he set out on his long journey, before he vanished for good. And when King Habbus dies, in his will he makes Samuel the Vizier of Granada. Three times seven is twenty-one; for that many years he is all but omnipotent in Granada! A Nagid, a prince—that's how they honored him, as Samuel haNagid—and poor Jews in their blindness believed that with him the words of the prophets had come true, that the era of the Jewish kingdom had arrived and they were about to enter the circle of power and authority! When he died, he was succeeded, as a matter of course, by his son Joseph. A dried flower pressed in book pages and gone moldy! Choking in his infinite knowledge, he entertained himself and his sycophantic court by issuing senseless orders. For example: Blue-eyed citizens must greet dark-eyed citizens by spreading their legs and showing their backsides. Or: Peasants, whether men or women, must taste the soil before sowing any seeds, and if they find the soil tasteless they must salt it. But even this did not satisfy Joseph. When he tired of his books, he would strip naked, saying that otherwise he couldn't see or believe or feel he had a body and when he was naked, a bell was sounded and everyone in the palace had to walk about naked, too. Ladies and gentlemen alike! Servants and soldiers! Tailors and petitioners! Well, you can imagine! After seven years of such rule, one windy night, on December 30 in the year 1066 according to the Christian calendar, infuriated Moors attacked the palace. Granada was in flames. Joseph was rushing down a corridor when they caught up with him, and silently murdered him as the dry wind fanned the curtains and the flames. His two children were taken along by people fleeing the palace. And thus, as the Lord had ordered, with these children begins the circle of suffering. They were twins, a boy and a girl, and very ugly. Their bodies were flabby and fat, their faces like baked apples that have rolled under the oven and begun to molder. After six years of wandering they reached Rouen, where a pious blind old Jew took them in. When did you last look in the mirror, Sarah'leh? Must be ten years, still in the palace, by accident. And you, Simon? I saw myself today, accidentally, while fishing in the lake. I look terrible. And why are you so beautiful? Because you love me, Shimeh'leh! And because I love you, too, you don't look terrible to me, on the contrary! The Almighty must have ordered things that way, so they wouldn't have to hide before the blind old man. They lived by begging, sitting on the steps of temples, and everybody gave them something because they looked so hideous that the sight of them struck horror in the hearts of healthy people. When left to themselves they hugged, pinched, and scratched each other, wildly and insatiably. As if the two monsters—don't forget these were your ancestors also!—wanted to melt into one body! The sick bodies were guided by healthy instincts. The boy got the girl with child. It was possible to make love and even to give birth in silence, but the newborn did cry out and the blind old man heard that. The Jews ran to the house of the beggar. The twins were chased out of the house, the newborn stayed. They hadn't even left Rouen when, by the city walls, the abominable mother was released from this life by a terrible fever and the father, husband to his own blood, hanged himself on a tree. Benjamin was the name they gave the newborn, but although they had it circumcised, no one could decide with absolute certainty whether it was a boy or a girl; it was hunchbacked and completely hairless when it grew up. And Benjamin did not know what sex he or she was. When left by itself, Benjamin was capable of embracing itself, and having gratified all its desires, it would kiss its own hands and tell itself joyously: I am superior to them! What there is separately in others I have together in me! In near delirium, Benjamin would daydream like this: What happiness it would be if I could give birth to my own child, one that I conceived all by myself! And if it weren't for the help of God, if God hadn't helped out at such a terrible cost, then with Benjamin, there and then, the whole thing would have ended, and then my great-grandfather couldn't have told the story in Sátoraljaújhely, and my grandfather in Szernye couldn't have told me about it under the mulberry tree, and I couldn't be telling you this here, right now. It was growing dark. It was the moment when the dimness of twilight is not quite ready to yield to the night and bides its time. The dull stamping of water buffaloes can be heard in the street. In mists exhaled by the nearby woods the nearby mountains slowly disappear. It was all very beautiful. Solemn. At dawn they sent Benjamin away, to Worms. Carrying a letter, avoiding cities and villages, sleeping under trees, Benjamin was on the road for several months." I couldn't help it, I stole a glance at Grandpapa. His eyes were closed and he was speaking so softly I don't think he could hear himself. I couldn't figure out what that popping sound was while he was talking, but then I realized that while he was telling me Benjamin's story, the roof tiles that had been so hot during the day were now cooling off. "I, Jehiel, serving our Lord and Father as Rabbi of Rouen, send my greetings to you and yours! Peace be unto you, my brethren! I wish to inform you, in case the news has not reached you, that at the Christian Council, convoked in Clermont in the spring of this year, Urban, leader of the Christians, declared war. Their purpose is to recover our ancient land, which they call a holy grave. They have been recruiting troops, and we have supplied the necessary monies—after careful consideration. But the Almighty has turned His will against us, and the weapons purchased with our money are being used first of all not to kill the distant Muslims but for the mass destruction of our people. The noble knights are now gathering around Rouen, clamoring for more loans; in giving them money we know that by this act we are signing our own death warrant. We cannot yet know for what sins the Lord is punishing us. I believe, my wise Gershon, rabbi in Worms, it is a dead man who is writing this letter to you. Therefore we ask you to meditate on these things, to pray and to fast! Thus read the letter brought by Benjamin to the Jews of Worms. Among the fourteen children of this Rabbi Gershon was a hunchbacked girl. It seems she had been waiting just for Benjamin. The rabbi promised a handsome dowry. The money interested Benjamin, but he was afraid: if he married, the secret of his sex would be revealed. But the girl was passionate. Even before the nuptials she spared no effort until, overcoming his doubts, the man in Benjamin won out. The newborn was only two days old—later, Benjamin's son said it was May 18—when Crusaders attacked the Jewish quarter. The woman fled with the baby, but Benjamin's mind clouded over with the knowledge that soldiers were coming; he dressed again as a woman. His body was cut into tiny slices, the earth drank his blood, and his flesh was devoured by hungry cats. The hunchbacked mother and the healthy baby, named David, sailed across the ocean. For fifteen years we lived in Norwich, and this is how we, having been German Ashkenazim, became English. Here, in Norwich, there was a boy, apprenticed to a skinner, who carried on a sinful liaison with his master's wife, but his master also played mischief with him; the boy's name was William. On Easter Eve William's dead body was found in the forests of Norwich. The Jews were accused of having murdered him so they could mix his blood into their unleavened bread for Pesach. The townspeople dragged the body in front of the synagogue; the wounds opened up and living blood gushed from the boy's heart. The Jewish quarter of Norwich went up in flames, just as the one in York was to burn forty-four years later. By then David, along with his children, was living in York. Among his children was one who took after his grandfather: a nearly blind, hunchbacked dwarf. Allegedly, in York, as the Easter procession passed along the street of the Jews, an old lady emptied the contents of a chamber pot—heaved out of the window, as usual—right on the image of the Madonna. The Jews fled to the castle of the bishop, who, being good and benevolent, stood on the parapet to reason with the armed, enraged mob: In the name of Jesus, stop! An arrow passed through his open mouth and came out at the back of his head. The castle of York was set afire by lobbed-in pitch and hemp, and when the Jews saw there was no escape, they lowered David's son, the hunchbacked Benjamin, in a basket. If we must perish, at least the news of our fate must live on! This brief sentence may serve as the motto of our descendants." I repeated it together with Grandpapa until I had learned it by heart and could say it by myself: "If we must perish, at least the news of our fate must live on! Listen! They wanted to live! To live, no matter what! My grandfather didn't say—he couldn't have known—but I am adding this: as if the disgrace of living could save you from death! And so followed the age of cunning. Feeling and reason degenerate completely, only the sheer will to live remains. Benjamin wandered for two whole years before reaching Erfurt. There his mouth delivered the message, but his hands were empty. The congregation was saddened by the news, and to help this sole survivor they made Benjamin a guard in the cemetery, paying him two years' salary in advance, a pretty nice sum, saying, Maybe you can do something with this money. Benjamin washed bodies, dug graves, got married, saved up. One child was born to him, a huge blond boy who earned the reputation of a rowdy and drank a lot, played dice, and kept a Christian mistress. Around that time the plague was spreading everywhere. Allegedly, it was Jews who contaminated the wells out of vengeance; Benjamin was washing chancrous, bluish, festering Jewish corpses, until the plague got him, too. Before losing consciousness, this is how he spoke to his blond son, whom he loved beyond words: Everything will be exactly as it has been until now! Everything will be repeated exactly as I tell it but in different forms. I know! In a few days Erfurt will burn, just as in the days of our forebears the cities of Cádiz, Granada, and Rouen burned, the way Worms, Norwich, and York burned! But this is where we left off, in York! When we could no longer hold the castle, the Jews collected all the money they had managed to rescue, and piled it into one big heap along with all their other valuables. This is the MONEY OF THE DEAD, they said, for though we're still living, we are as good as dead. And because you are the craftiest one among us, pass this on to the LIVING. And ask them to pray. That's when I fled with the treasure to Erfurt. But I didn't pass it on then, I am giving it to you now. I'm not dishonest, because you are one of the living, too. But I don't have enough time to tell you my whole adventure-filled story. Behind the cemetery is a solitary oak, you know the tree. If you dig a hole, do it at night, three steps north of the tree's trunk and about two feet deep, and you'll find everything, together with what I have saved since then. My dear child, I speak to you from my deathbed: no more wine, no more drinking, don't drink! And with the treasure go to Vienna and look for Henel, who will give you good advice. And now, I will bless you. My father was crying and I was ashamed because my eyes were dry, but I knew it would be hypocritical to pretend I'd give up my pleasures. In Vienna a servant stood in front of Henel's house. I told him, Go, tell your master that Jacob Mendel from Erfurt, son of Benjamin, would like to talk to him. Henel received Jacob Mendel standing up. He wanted to know how much Jacob wished to invest in business. Jacob named half the sum of his capital. But just how much that was he never revealed to anyone, not even to his son, so nobody could pass on the information. Henel mentally multiplied the sum by three, smacked his lips in approval, and knew that if he were to send his own son to Buda, he would give him four times as much, so that Jacob Mendel's son would not be richer than Henel's. Henel, having clicked his tongue a few more times, put a paternal hand on Jacob's shoulder and his eyes welled up: I do feel sorry for you, my child, for being an orphan! I also have a son, about your age, and I can imagine how he would weep if he were to lose me forever. My poor, poor boy! But don't stay in Vienna! Vienna is small and here I control everything. And your wealth is ridiculously small, I'd say it's not worth shit. But I would suggest that you go to Buda. The King of Hungary has just issued his *census iudeorum*: a great new golden opportunity for Jews. Freedom for gold, eh! My own son is moving there, why not go with him! Be his friend, his brother. And at this point the age of cunning makes way for the age of rivalry and combativeness. In Buda. Or maybe we should say that cunning put on a combat uniform? The year: 1251 according to the Christian calendar. We don't know exactly what happened, or how. It's a business secret. But within a few years that seem like a few seconds, the Mendels are lords of Buda. They are tall, blond, harsh-faced. They build their own houses and a big synagogue. In all the surrounding streets—construction is going on everywhere—only co-religionists live, money changers, pawnbrokers, and merchants. With borrowed money many Frenchmen, Germans, Italians, and also a few Hungarians build beautiful homes in Buda. And Jacob begat Solomon. Solomon's son was Judah. And Judah begat a son named Joseph. They all lived long lives. One afternoon, when he is already old, Joseph makes the son of his son sit next to him. They are looking out at the river, with its drifting, crunching ice floes, and the grandfather tells the following story: One bright Sunday King Matthias arrived in Buda. At his side his young wife, Beatrix. We received him on horseback, as the other lords did, but in a separate group. Thirty-one splendid Jewish riders in parade formation. Up front, on a white steed, was your father, and he blew a beautiful tune on his trumpet. He was followed by ten young lads on pitch-black stallions, silver belts around their waists, with buckles big enough to be goblets. Long swords in silver scabbards at their sides, the gold hilts studded with precious jewels. Commanding the detachment, I rode behind them in simple gray formal attire; that's how I had planned it: mine should be simple and formal. On my head I wore a velvet-lined peaked hat, a reminder to the king that Jews in other countries had to wear this kind of hat as a sign of humiliation, but my silversmith, who could hold his own against our Rufus, had ornamented the hat with silver, and in a plain gold scabbard I had the most beautiful of all my swords. Behind me my entourage rode in pairs; on their hats ostrich feathers fluttered, they all wore maroon dress uniforms, and under a silk canopy they carried the Laws of Moses. Then came two armed riders, and finally the servants bearing the gifts I would later present to the queen. The dazzling royal pair stopped at the palace parade ground, by the well. Here, while Judah played his trumpet, I handed them two loaves of bread, a beautiful hat with ostrich feathers, two big stags and two deer, tied up, eight peacocks, and a number of expensive decorative kerchiefs, twelve to be exact; then two men presented the chief part of our gift: a basket woven of silver threads and filled with twenty pounds of pure silver. After Judah came Jacob, to whom his grandfather, Joseph, told the story on a winter evening. After Jacob another Jacob; after him Judah—the Jewish prefects. Their rule was inherited by Israel Mendel, then Isaac Mendel, but by Isaac's time the Turks were at Mohács. The news comes in the evening: the battle is lost, the queen is widowed, everyone who can run or walk is fleeing; this is the thirtieth day of August. They gather in the great hall, where old Isaac, who will die that same night, speaks to them like this: We have been through many experiences. Experiences of all the ages are in our blood. Our instinct is to flee. Still, I say we should stay put, the Turks are clever, and we are no fools. Isaac's son, Moses, on a cushion, takes the keys to the city of Buda to Suleiman. Isaac's idea has saved us. But in September the sultan summons them. As they enter, they see Suleiman seated on a dais; having just returned from a hunt, his face is reddened by the wind and he is twirling his long beard; as is the custom, they fall to their knees and in that position listen to what he has to say: My sweet ones! I shall leave this country to its fate. And what I have not done will be accomplished by two ignorant rivals: not even grass will grow here. And that is how the country will fall to me tomorrow, with no effort on my part. Let me quote a Turkish proverb, my sweet ones: Two swords don't fit into one scabbard, and there is no room for two lions in one cave. I hope you understand me. Between two swords, between two lions, what will be your fate? Therefore, come with me. Besides, I won't allow you to stay. What I respect is the sweet things in life. And money, clinking and jingling, provided it clinks and jingles for me. Do you understand me? We shall be happy together! Moses Mendel replied with a Jewish proverb: If the people knew what others intended to do for them, they'd commit suicide! Your Majesty, Sire, I hope you understand: we are mere delegates of the people. The pashas winced. Moses Mendel's head was parted from his body. Then, crammed into the belly of a boat, the Jews floated down the Danube. Their houses were looted and set on fire; but Moses' younger son, disguised as a beggar, secretly stayed on in Buda. The other son, the older one, is in Constantinople, studying Turkish. So don't be surprised if in your dreams you find yourself speaking Turkish. The sighs of the two brothers drift toward each other across the great distance. And when the Janissaries set the synagogues on fire and Constantinople is burning, Moses's son Abraham returns to Buda. The two brothers meet again. Jews from many other places also make their way to Buda. Abraham's son is capable and clever; his wealth is not great, but sufficient. In Gershon's store many items of the Far East are available. And his son, Dan, is famous for his physical prowess, and behold, another hundred years have run down the infinite circle of time. The imperial troops of the Holy Roman Emperor come to liberate Buda; Dan takes the side of the Turks, fighting valiantly, and he is the one who exclaims what has become my motto: Let us die, so that we may be saved! Fighting and annihilation are cousins. Annihilation is the failure of fighting, and there's no man on earth who understands that better than I. Because the circle of annihilation is my circle. And yours, too? Or have you stepped into another one? This we cannot tell, not yet. On the second of September Buda was burning and so was the synagogue where the elderly, the women, and the children sought refuge; the walls came tumbling down. Again a moment when it all could have ended. But I can go on! Don't ask why. Now comes the miracle! In the ranks of the Imperials had been someone as valiant as Dan who fell, as a hero, in the great battle. This man's name is Alexander Simon! Does the name sound familiar? Yes! He's the one! A descendant of the very Simon who had stayed in Jerusalem when Rufus left for Rome. And this is where the divided family, which had been going in two different directions, gets united again. Dan, who died, leaves behind a most beautiful daughter whose name is Esther. The girl escapes from the synagogue, her dress on fire, her lovely black hair singed. Embracing her in his strong arms, Alexander puts out the flames of her dress. And it is also Alexander Simon who pays ransom, simply buys from the emperor the one hundred and forty surviving Jews. The defeated army heads for Nicolsburg, but for Alexander and Esther the retreat is a bridal procession. From Nicolsburg, if you must run away, the road leads to Prague. And from Prague, when they have to escape, their children again set foot on Hungarian soil, and their name is Simon once more. Kőszeg is their home, and then Pest for a while, and then follows the period of peacefulness. The sixth circle of the story. After Pest comes Kassa, or Kosice, then Sátoralja-újhely. That's where Abraham Simon, the miracle rabbi, lives, whose company was sought even by the young Lajos Kossuth, because my grandfather gave everybody wise counsel. And it was my grandfather who moved here, to Szernye; by then my father was alive. We've had this house ever since, and it's been getting larger and larger, who knows how big it'll get? and this mulberry tree, too. That's the story of our family. Since the destruction of Jerusalem it has traversed six of the infinite number of circles. How will it do with the seventh? That I don't know. Perhaps after peacefulness will come happiness, at last. And maybe that will be yours, a great gift from God, after so much trouble. In the meantime, our wealth has dwindled, along with our taste for combat. But we have enough not to starve, and we are still alive, and we go on living. I still feel I'm rich: I have not only all those years—which are now yours, too!—but also God, whom I thought I had lost but then found again. And these years, well, here you are, I am giving them to you. But God you'll have to win for yourself, if He so wills it and if you can. That's when my grandfather stopped talking. The moon rose, red, over the mountains. It was as if I were rising. He didn't know it yet.

In me the final annihilation was to come. Will it be your share, too? That I don't know. Leaning out the window my grandmother saw the evening star in the sky; it was suppertime. And she called out, Yoohoo! Let's go, said my grandfather. Some other time I'll tell you the rest, what's still left over. And the family sat down to supper."

"*Ecce homo!*" shouted Grandpapa, and threw the fish on the table. "Behold the man! Just imagine: it could easily be a man. Man may sometimes have an inkling of what is about to happen to him, that's the only difference. But who can tell what inkling a fish has? And with so much air around, it can scarcely breathe. Well, I certainly can't tell." Grandmama handed Grandpapa the mallet she used for tenderizing meat; he should knock it dead with that. "But, Papa, please be careful! don't break the tiles!" Grandpapa laughed. The fish was thrashing, opening and closing its mouth and its gills. "You heard that? women are so humane! She wouldn't do the actual killing. Oh no, because she's such a gentle soul! But she's strong enough to be the instigator, isn't she? It's my hands that have to put out a life while she—what is she doing? She worries about the table-top!" Grandpapa grabbed the fish, but it jumped and slid from his hand. Grandmama covered her eyes. Grandpapa brought down the mallet. "Your hand, watch your hand, Papa!" I could see her peeking from between her fingers. The head cracked, but the fish was still alive, flinging itself about, smearing the tabletop with its slippery goo. "One more shot and it will be all over. Unfortunately, the eyes popped out with the first blow. So the soup won't taste so good. Fish soup is tastier if the eyes are in it." "Should I make soup out of it?" "If it has roe or milk, yes, add the tail and head—but let's not forget to take out its bitter tooth, that flat tooth behind the gills!—and you can make a nice tart little soup from it." "I'll fry the rest." "Or you can bake it with flour and paprika. Today my stool was normal. Well, then, one last time!" Grandpapa raised the mallet and delivered the blow. The fish wasn't sliding around any more, only its tail was twitching a little. "Here before us lies a dead body. A carp, also known as *Cyprinus carpio*, just as the Latin name for man is *Homo sapiens*. Before opening it up, let us take a look at its exterior. It's fishlike. Its form is functional, enabling it to live in its environment. Except I don't know what the first fish that lived in water looked like. Not quite as fish-like as this? Did it adapt gradually? Or when God created lifeless water did He simultaneously create its living mate, the fishlike fish? Mama, if you please, give us a nice sharp pointed knife! The body of the fish, as you can see, is longish. It belongs to the family of vertebrates. It is thinnest along the spine, its belly, with its vital organs, is the most bulging or convex part. These are the gills, the organ of respiration. Its blood, as you can see, is red, like human blood, only it's not warm but cold. Its skin is covered with scales, laid one on top of the other, from below upward, like the tiles of a roof. If we want to take the tiles off a roof, we have to start on top, at the spine. We, on the other hand, will insert the sharp blade here, at the tail, under the tiles, you see, that's the easiest way to get them all off, from below upward. The equivalent for the fish of your arms and legs are fins. With its tail fin and breast fins it propels itself forward, and this collapsible lobe behind this thorn on its back determines the direction it swims in. But how does the fish rise to the surface or sink to the bottom, if it wants to? With the help of its abdominal fins. These, here. You can see that in its exterior everything is functional and well arranged. And who or what arranged it like this? And when? I don't know! And you should also know that contrary to their reputation, fish have excellent hearing; a fish has no external ears, as humans do, but it need not register such a wide range of sounds. There is a certain muted quality that goes along with the world it lives in. With its mouth and with the nerves all along the lateral line, here, these pores on its sides, it feels things. It can also smell. Here are the nostrils. Its mouth is lined with mucus membranes, good for tasting things. It probably sees well the things that are important for it to see. But how a fish eye sees the fish world, well, we simply don't know enough to tell. And you can imagine how unpleasant it might be for someone to be reborn in a next life as a fish. He will always be seeing things. For him there will be no day and no night. Because the fish has no eyelids. It can't close its eyes, it has nothing to close them with. Maybe that's why the fish are so wise. They produce no sound. Maybe that's why they live so long. There is a hundred-and-fifty-year-old carp that lives in Charlottenburg, and just this year it wrote a letter to Uncle Frigyes, telling him that it was still feeling pretty good. When Frigyes comes over, ask him what his friend wrote to him! Maybe it'll live to be two hundred. And now let's open it up and look inside! However unpleasant it is, I have to begin here, in its ass." "Papa! Watch your language!" "This hole is the end of the intestinal canal, this is where the fish evacuates. Fitting the knife in there makes it easy to open the fish. But this bone, which holds the two breast fins together, makes dissection a bit harder. But it's the correct way! And the knife is sharp! We move on easily all the way to the head. Now we could actually cut its head off. Put it aside and we'll examine it separately. Too bad, I can see already that it has neither roe nor milk. Forget the fish soup! Put your hand in there! Don't be scared! Fish is one of your most immediate ancestors, like Grandmama's or mine, too, because in our mother's womb, we are fish for a few weeks; it's like the dark sea bottom, can you feel it? The contents of your stomach is very much like that, too. Now take your hand out. We have to be careful how to tear things out: if the gallbladder bursts and its contents spill out, it turns the meat bitter, this, this dark green thing. With the tip of the knife we remove it nicely, and now we can freely poke around in all the rest. This is the liver, the intestines, this is the heart, and this one's the stomach. The kidney leads into the opening of the cloaca; the fish pees at the same place it poops. And now we nicely ask Grandmama not to grumble but to give us a bowl with some water in it. And now let's take a look at the head. This here is the softest spot, like our neck, it's easy to cut it up. Thank you. In the meantime, let the body swim, if it can! Tap the top of the head! Hard, eh? Inside, a hollow, that's where the brain is. Not much, but enough, more or less, for the fish to manage. Smartly we peel off the disks of the gills, you'll see how beautiful what's under it is, this thing, pretty hard. These crimson arches! You couldn't live in water because you wouldn't be able to breathe. And the fish would drown on shore. Let me explain. There is oxygen in the water, in the air, too. The fish takes in water through its mouth, the water rushes through these fine little crimson disks in which blood circulates, the blood sniffs up the oxygen out of the water, and the circulation takes it to the heart. That's the heart! It has two parts, one's called the auricle, the other is the ventricle. The blood is freshened up by the oxygen, and the heart pumps the fresh blood into every part of the fish's body. The fish lives in water like a fish in water, does all sorts of fishy things which tire the blood, and through the veins the tired blood returns to the heart; the heart pumps the bad blood back here, among the little disks, that's when the cover rises! and the used oxygen that's no longer oxygen goes back into the water. Now comes the ugliest little operation. Cutting it up into pieces. If you take this float, also called the air bladder, and put it out in the sun to dry, you can hit it and it'll give you a nice loud pop. Here you are. Go ahead, take it. In the meantime, Grandmama will prepare the fish." I went out into the garden. The sun was shining. The dog was lying in its house, its muzzle sticking out, sleeping. I squatted down and shoved the bladder under its nose; it jerked its head and opened its eyes. It wanted to eat the bladder, snapped at it, but I ran away and the dog followed me, jumping around my hand. I ran to the gate, wanted to put the bladder in the mailbox, where the dog couldn't get at it. There were no letters in the box, it was empty. Two white butterflies came along, chasing each other, I ran after them to see if they were doing what flies do. And the dog was running after me. The butterflies disappeared in the blue space above the bushes. A rustling noise. Éva was sitting under one of the bushes, pretending to be crying. I picked up a stone and threw it at the dog, get out of here; it put its tail between its legs and ran off, but kept looking back. I threw another stone after him. "Oh, my husband is dead! What's to become of me? Why did he have to go away?" I knew now, she was playing the Mama, Gábor the Papa, and I could only be the child again. "Oh, oh my God! who will cook supper for him in his death?" "His mistress will!" "There are no mistresses in death!" "And he didn't even die! He's standing on the terrace!" Éva took her hands away from her eyes. "What are you doing here? Did anybody ask you to come? Idiot!" And I showed her the bladder, but she shoved me and the bladder fell out of my hand, she grabbed it and crawled out of the bush through the hole toward their garden. But I caught her foot, wouldn't let her take the bladder. "That's mine!" I was pulling her foot, but with her other foot she kicked me. I was crying, but also noticed the play of little spots of light in the bush.

Grandmama was calling for me. While we were eating the fish, the telephone rang in the hallway. Grandmama ran out to answer it, but we didn't hear who she was talking to. She called to Grandpapa. I kept eating my fish. Grandpapa said to be careful with the bones. Grandmama told me that once, in her house, before her father was trampled to death by the horse when he fell off the carriage, on Friday evening they were eating fish when suddenly they saw that her father's face had turned blue. As if life had gone out of him, he couldn't breathe and just sat there. Everybody was shouting. And then she remembered what somebody had told her, it was Béla Zöld, that when a fishbone gets stuck in somebody's throat they should slap his back and that would make him cough and the bone either comes back up or goes down. She slapped her father's back and the bone came up, and they continued eating. But when they finished, my mother got up and slapped me in the face and shouted, How dare you hit your father? I laughed, because I tried to imagine Grandmama getting slapped in the face. But Grandpapa said, "What are you laughing at? Do you have any idea what you're doing when you laugh? You know what that is?" "No, I don't." "There, you see? Laughing is one of life's greatest mysteries." But I waited in vain, they didn't come back to the table. I wasn't eating the fish any more, it was very quiet in the house. Grandpapa's chair was still where he had kicked it out from under him when he got up. I heard no noise from the hallway either. On Grandmama's plate I saw the long skeleton with bits of fish still on one side, and on the rim of the plate all the little bones she had spat out. I walked through the rooms. Grandpapa was sitting in his armchair. Grandmama was lying in her bed. I watched her to see whether she was breathing. Now I could steal the candy from under her pillow. The candy stuck to the bag, I had to spit out the paper. The man was standing in the doorway. "Béla! Come quick! Béla! Hurry up! We've got a body here, really!" The voice is coming closer, the floor is creaking. I did have a magnifying glass at home. "Grandmama managed to get fish." "You don't have to clean it, because I must leave early in the morning." "Could I sleep with you then, Father?" "Hey, I almost forgot! Give me my pants. You see this? If you hold it in the sun, it concentrates all the beams and the paper catches on fire. You can try it tomorrow." Outside, the wind is blowing even though the sun was shining only a little while ago. Pearls are running down the side of the sputtering candle. "If you look at something through this, you can see the tiniest details. You see? That's the kind of little hills and valleys you have on your skin." Grandpapa was sitting in the armchair. If I could breathe along with him. Something is happening, but I don't know what. I don't. What is this? A buzzing from the direction of the window. Maybe if I look at it through the new magnifying glass. A fly was caught in the cobweb. It wants to get away and the spider is at the edge of the web. It's the fly buzzing. Its legs are stuck in the web, no use flapping its wings. Grandpapa was sitting in the armchair. I had a magnifying glass, I used it to watch when I killed a spider or a fly. Afternoon. He pressed his palms between his knees and slept. His mouth was open, his dentures on the table. I was listening to his breathing and observed that when I sit with him like that for a long time then the air goes in and out of my mouth at the same slow rate as does his. Grandmama was calling from upstairs: "Papa! Papa! Come right away! Papa!" Grandpapa closed his mouth, looked at me, and made little sucking sounds. "What is it? Is something wrong? My teeth!" Grandmama wouldn't let up, she kept calling. All the doors were open to create a little draft. "Papa! Papa! Come quick! It's Feri talking!" I ran ahead and Grandpapa dropped his cane and I didn't pick it up for him, and he held on to the furniture and doors. "Papa, Papa, quick! He's talking already! He's saying his name now! Papa!" Grandmama was calling at the top of the stairs and on the radio somebody was talking. Grandpapa stopped at the bottom of the stairs, I ran halfway up. "Papa! Papa! Feri's talking on the radio!" Grandmama ran back and turned up the volume so Grandpapa could hear the radio downstairs. "Let me warn you that you may have to take an oath on your statement; so please tell the truth. False testimony is punished severely by the law. Do you understand?" "Yes." "Papa, that's him!" "Please tell us where, how, and in what circumstances you learned that the accused was to meet Henry Bundren, a spy working for the American secret service. And tell us also what role you played in arranging this meeting." "If I remember correctly, on July 13 or 14 of this year I was instructed by Regimental Commander Pál Suhajda that, as an intelligence officer of the regiment, at an appropriate location—" "Papa! Feri is talking! Papa!" "Please tell us exactly how it took place, in full detail." "Yes. At the above-mentioned time Colonel Pál Suhajda called me in and told me the following: a high-ranking member of the government has arranged a meeting, through diplomatic channels, with a high-ranking official of the Yugoslav government. You are familiar with the deterioration in Hungarian-Yugoslav relations. Our task is to keep this meeting in the strictest—" "Papa! Feri! That's Feri!" "Be quiet!" "I put you in charge of solving the technical problems of the task, and regarding the proper location I want your report at five o'clock this afternoon, so that I can pass it on immediately to Comrade Commander of the Political Group. This is approximately what he told me. I took the necessary measures, and that same afternoon, sometime before five o'clock, I reported back that three kilometers from the town of Gyékényes, near the border, was an abandoned building surrounded by an acacia forest, which locals called the Buchel farm. I also reported to Suhajda that if it was necessary I could have the place furnished overnight." "What happened next?" "Although I had long harbored suspicions of the colonel, this matter could not be suspect since he had mentioned the involvement of Comrade Commander of the Political Group who, I thought, certainly at the time, to be above suspicion." "Let me warn you that you were asked simply to answer the question: What happened next? Refrain from comments and stick to the facts." "Yes. The next thing that happened was that the colonel sent me out and told me to wait in the secretary's office. All I can tell you is that in the meantime he spoke to Budapest, on a direct line, and the conversation lasted approximately twenty minutes." "How does the witness know that Suhajda was talking to Budapest, and on a direct line?" "While in the secretary's office, talking to the secretary, I noticed which line signaled 'busy' on the telephone on her desk. And everyone knew on which line one could talk only with Budapest." "All right. Carry on." "Then the colonel called me back into his office and told me that in light of the urgency of the matter, I should arrange for cleaning and furnishing the farm immediately, because in all probability the meeting would take place within twenty-four hours.

Comrade Commander of the Political Group ordered that the furnishings be the simplest possible. He instructed me to take a conference table with a green felt cover from the quartermaster's or, if there wasn't one there, to get a table like that from anywhere, and also some chairs. And I should have the walls whitewashed if they were dirty. I asked if I should see about some decoration, he said, no, there was no need, but there must be a working latrine." "What other instructions were you given?" "I was instructed that immediately after completion of the job, the detachment setting up the house be ordered to their summer quarters, where, in complete isolation, they should be kept busy with disciplinary, bordering on punitive, exercise. The colonel laughed at this and said it was a brilliant idea, because at least that way the men would even forget who their mother was." "I warn the witness to tell the whole truth. According to police records, the colonel laughed at this because it was the witness's idea." "Yes, I beg your pardon. It was my idea, and the colonel approved it." "Go on." "I was instructed that the whole area must be secured within a few hours, but the troops doing the job should not be allowed to see the meeting site and must not know what sort of task they were performing. The colonel put me in charge of the company. Movement within the secured area was possible only with the right password given at designated times. I myself was not allowed inside the security ring. This arrangement, the colonel said, he would supervise personally. And then he said that we should start without delay, which we did. And by the way, I kept him informed, in detail, of every stage of our progress. Except for one matter. As I've already mentioned, Suhajda's activities had seemed questionable to me since about the beginning of the year. In this case my suspicion was aroused by the speed with which this had to be organized. Also, so far as I knew, important discussions between governments were not usually held in such places. Negotiations of this kind are usually arranged more easily, the governments concerned working through their respective foreign representatives in a neutral country. But what made me most suspicious was this: if what Suhajda had told me was indeed to take place, then, given the political tension at the time, he would surely have had that telephone conversation in front of me, so that I could hear it. As a counter-intelligence officer, I was authorized to hear such things; as a matter of fact, Comrade Minister of the Interior had expressly instructed me to follow the commander's activities closely, if I thought it was necessary. For this reason I ordered a soldier from Unit V to hide in the attic of the farm, to take down in shorthand every word he might hear, and to give his notes only to me; in no circumstance was he to leave the place until I personally came to get him. I found this soldier particularly well suited for the job because he was politically mature and an excellent stenographer." "What was the name of this soldier?" "Tamás Kolozsvári." "Spelled with an *i* or a *y* at the end?" "With an *i*, I think." "The court, at its convenience, will cross-examine this Tamás Kolozsvári. Please go on." "The meeting took place on the night of July 15. I myself was not within the security ring, therefore I have direct knowledge only of the following: at about ten-thirty in the evening, a black sedan came from the direction of Gyékényes and stopped on the road leading to the farm, with its headlights off. Somebody opened the door and gave the password to the soldiers standing at both sides of the road. It was a dark night. The farmhouse was lit only with a signal lamp by which the arrivals could orient themselves." "What kind of lamp?" "A kerosene lamp, at one end of the porch." "Do you have any knowledge as to where and how Henry Bundren crossed the border?" "No. I have no knowledge of that. I was only given a report that two men arrived, gave the password, and reached the house." "Now tell us what happened the following day." "The next day Tamás Kolozsvári reported that his notes were rather incomplete because he had had to jot them down in complete darkness, though he had heard everything very clearly. I myself went to get him, after I had the security ring lifted and the company had left for their summer quarters. While still in the car, Kolozsvári told me that the foreigner had spoken in English and used an interpreter. I managed to get Kolozsvári unnoticed into my office, where in a few hours he transcribed and typed up his notes." "How many pages?" "Fifteen. And it was indeed rather incomplete." "Did you read it?" "Yes. I did." "What were its contents?" "Among other things it said that the Yugoslav instructions ought to be carried out as if they had come directly from the CIA. But the most shocking part was the section dealing with how Comrades Rákosi and Gerő were to be assassinated." "Stop. The notes are in the court's possession. Tell us what you did after that." "For a few hours I was completely helpless because I couldn't think of a pretext for going to Budapest. I wouldn't have dreamed of using the telephone, because by then it was clear that even the direct line was at the espionage agency's disposal. But luck came to my aid. I received a telegram from my mother telling me that my eighty-four-year-old father had died during the night, and asking me to come home immediately. Because of the telegram Suhajda let me go to Budapest. In fact, I had the impression that he was decidedly glad I was going. Here I came directly to party headquarters and gave the material to the head of the Administrative Department. I asked him to have reservist Kolozsvári transferred out immediately, since, besides me, he was the only one who knew everything, and through him the conspirators might get wind of their impending exposure. He took action immediately and within half an hour told me that for the sake of absolute security the authorities had arrested Kolozsvári, who had already been on his way to Budapest. After that I went home and awaited further instructions." "Does any member of the people's tribunal have any questions for the witness? The people's prosecutor? The defense? Accused! Have you any observations?" "None." "Please, take the accused prisoners away. The court will continue its work after a short recess." Grandmama left the room. I got up from the steps. Grandpapa let go of the banister he'd been holding on to. Grandmama came down the stairs and I fell in behind her. "Why did he say such a thing? He didn't come home, then! Papa! Why? Why don't you answer me? Why did he say such a thing, when you're alive? Papa!" "Could I have been wrong?" Upstairs you could hear the radio still saying something, then music came on. Grandmama got hold of Grandpapa's hand. "Papa!" "Could I have been wrong?" "Papa, why do you keep saying that? Please say something, I can't stand it any more! Papa!" "Could I have been wrong?" Grandpapa started for their room, and it looked as if he was leading Grandmama. His cane was on the floor in my room. He kicked it and the cane slid all the way to the wall. Grandpapa sat in the armchair. Pressing his two hands between his knees, he was asleep. His mouth was open and he was breathing loudly, as though something was stuck in his throat. I was careful not to listen to his breathing and maybe fall asleep like him. When Grandmama called him because lunch was ready, he woke up and smacked his lips. He took his denture from the windowsill and put it into his mouth. "Yes. I believe so." "What, what do you believe Papa!" "Could I have been wrong?" But he did show up for supper. Supper, too, was eaten in silence; only when he got up and looked at Grandmama did Grandpapa say something: "Tell me, Mama!" "What? My dear, talk to me!" "Could I have been wrong?" "About what? What are you thinking about? Aren't you going to tell me?" "Yes. I think so. Could I have been wrong?" They closed the door and the bed creaked, and Grandmama kept asking Grandpapa, but to no avail. And then the crack under the door went dark, too. The window was open and I kicked off the cover. "Is this a cricket?" "No, son, unfortunately it's already a cicada, a harvest fly." I tried to walk without making the floor creak. I went into that room, turned on the light, and opened the closet door. The smell of lavender in the closet. The lavender was in small white bags on the top shelf and on the bottom. I stopped to listen if Grandmama was coming, because I heard a creaky noise. Quickly I turned off the light and shut the closet door. But it was only the house, creaking all by itself. There was a small box at the very bottom of the closet and I didn't know what was in it. I pulled it out and all the rest of the boxes fell out of the closet. I stopped and listened again, but I was the only one who'd heard the boxes fall. In that box, folded nicely, a green velvet dress. Its top made of silk with tulle. I took off my pajamas and stood there naked. I pulled on the dress; it was very long. I thought of giving it to Éva. I was scared: If Grandmama comes in now I won't have time to put it back, and if she asks what I'm doing here, I'll tell her I forgot to brush my teeth. On the shelf in the bathroom we had a pair of scissors. With it I cut the gray disks out of the dress. I showed them to Éva and Gábor and lied that they were made of gold and our ancestors had left them here for us, only they painted them gray so nobody would know what they are. Gábor didn't believe it. He tapped one of them against his teeth and said it was lead and could be melted down. Whoever could roll the disk from the door all the way under the sofa was the winner. The door opened and their mother, all naked, walked across the room. In the next room she turned on the radio and we could hear that same voice as before. She put on the same silk robe Éva usually fooled around in whenever their mother was out for one of her appearances. She looked at herself in the mirror and listened to what was being said on the radio. Gábor accidentally slashed the armchair with the sword. She came back, wearing the robe, and sat down in the same chair. She watched the disks rolling. When I went home, Grandpapa was sitting in his armchair. He held out his hand, I went over to him and he hugged me. I could see his eyes from very close. "Could I have been wrong? Dead myths are the most lasting ones! Do you think so, too? Yes. Could I have been wrong?" And in his winter coat he was standing in the middle of the room. But I knew that this room was unfamiliar to me. Somebody was shouting. "If you cut your finger with a knife, it will hurt, won't it? That's how I cut into you, like a knife!" I jumped up and ran toward him, but he was receding. "It will hurt!" Suddenly he was here, very close. His eyes. I put my arms around his neck, and thought my crying would make him feel good. But when I pressed my face to his I felt its stubbles, because he shaved only every other day; he'd just gotten home and Grandmama hadn't cleaned his clothes yet. And I sat up again and realized I'd dreamed this whole thing. This is my bed. Or maybe this is a dream, too. This is my room, with the dark shadows of the trees in front of the window, and my father is not standing in the middle of the room. Something is strange. Grandpapa's breathing. But not strange in the usual way. The crack under the door is dark. Why is he breathing so loudly? As if something is stuck in his throat, wanting to come out but can't. It's just gurgling there, really loud. I listened in front of the door. I could see, in the dark, a body moving under the covers. "Grandpapa!" No answer, only the movement. "Grandpapa!" Grandmama was wheezing softly, but I couldn't see her bed because it was too dark. "Grandmama!" She didn't answer. Grandpapa's mouth is open. "Grandmama!" "What is it? What happened? What do you want?" "Grandmama!" Grandpapa's breathing turned into a whistle after each gurgle. "Papa! What is it? Papa!" Grandpapa didn't answer, his mouth was open, and I thought his eyes were focusing. "Papa! Answer me! What is it? My little papa! My dear! Answer me! Sweetest! What is it? My God! The doctor!! What is it? The doctor! What is it? Why?" Grandmama was running in the dark and I after her, with her. We were running around, all over the place. The edges of the furniture were only a distant pain. "Papa, what hurts? My dearest! Is anything hurting you? Oh, I have to get dressed! The doctor! I have to phone. Frigyes! Oh my God! Frigyes, Frigyes, he too, already! Oh God! Papa! I must telephone!" And now Grandpapa is doing the same thing, only faster. In the sudden light I press my hand against my eyes. Grandmama runs out of the room. It sounds as if something is sloshing around inside him, in his chest, making that gurgling sound. His mouth is open and his eyes are looking ahead, and in his fists he crumples the bedcover over his chest. And he closed his mouth and something bloody got squeezed out and trickled down from the two corners of his mouth, and on his face I saw purple spots. In the bathroom I wet a towel, thinking that this was what a compress was and if I put it on his head he'd be saved. But the telephone didn't work. Grandmama yanked a dress from the closet. With the towel she wiped the thing off his mouth, and now Grandpapa's mouth was shut and the compress seemed to have calmed him down, because he lay motionless. "Don't leave him for a second! The medicine!" Grandmama ran back in. She tried to force the heart drops into Grandpapa's mouth, but they dripped down at the side of his lips. "Don't leave him alone for a second!" I would have liked to hold his hand, but didn't dare. Fingers open, his hands were resting at his side and the pillow was wet around his head, and his forehead and hair were also wet. The gate slammed. Grandpapa opened his eyes again, as if he was listening, and his mouth opened, too, as if he was about to speak. And then he stayed that way. I ran to my room, to the window, to see when Grandmama was coming back. She must be running by the big cross, but it's hard for her because it's steep there. But the gate slammed again. She probably stopped by the cross and turned back because she forgot something. Grandmama covered the mirror with a black kerchief. His eyes couldn't be closed any more, and his chin dropped, though she tied it up. When it started to get light outside, she closed the shutters so it would stay dark inside. A candle was burning at Grandpapa's head, sputtering. Grandmama told me to stay there while she went to the church to arrange the funeral. He kept lying in the same position. Didn't notice the fly landing on his eyes. Have to shoo it away! Grandpapa's mouth was so dark and so deep, I thought he was empty inside. In the cemetery the wind was blowing a fire like the flame of huge candles. The coffin vanished in the deep hole, and clumps of earth reverberated on the lid as if it were empty, as if Grandpapa weren't inside it. When we came back from the cemetery we found the garden gate open, and the door to the house and all the doors inside the house were open, too, and through the open doors we saw Grandpapa sitting in the armchair. Grandmama held on to the doorknob. But I saw it wasn't Grandpapa but my father in Grandpapa's housecoat. He was asleep. Grandmama sat down. He woke up and we looked at one another, from a distance. "How did you get here?" Grandmama asked in a low voice. "I'm not working there any more. They forwarded the telegram, but I wasn't even in my new place yet and it waited for me there for another two days," he said. Grandmama stood up and went to her room. He got up, too. "What have you done?" Grandmama asked. "What?" he asked. "Take off that coat, and leave our room," said Grandmama. He left. Nobody said a word all day. I went outside to take a look at the leaf that stirs even when there's no wind. It was stirring then, too, I don't know why. In the evening, when we went to bed, he went past my room on the way to Grandmama. I wanted to hear them, but they spoke very quietly. I ran back to bed when he was on his way out. "You want me to tell you a story?" "No! I don't want you to." He sat down at the edge of my bed and pulled my head into his lap. Then I would have liked him to tell me a story, but it was also good just being there like that, in the silence; strange how he didn't breathe like Grandpapa even though he was his son. "Grandpapa told me stories of all our ancestors, but about his father—who's your grandfather, right? like Grandpapa with me, right?—about him he never said anything." "My grandfather? You want me to tell you about him? All right. Let's see, what shall I tell you about him? Let's start with this. They had an apartment in Hold Street, the whole second floor, a very large apartment. I was afraid of him. He was a small man with a beard and mustache. We also had a great-uncle who was his brother and lived with them because he was a bachelor, never married. Uncle Ernő. I loved Uncle Ernő more than my grandfather. Meals were always around a big table. Father sat at one end of it, Uncle Ernő at the other. During lunch they were always shouting; they were continuing some old political debate, because a long time ago, before I was born, they had spent their mornings in Parliament, on opposite sides, because one of them, my grandfather, belonged to the Tisza Party, while Uncle Ernő's idol was Kossuth. And back then, a long time ago, they would come home in separate carriages and, so I heard, would go on fighting just as they were always fighting around the table. After lunch, after he had done all the shouting he wanted, Grandfather went to sleep, but Uncle Ernő would sit around smoking his pipe and tell the craziest stories. Once, I remember, he told me that in Paris he had a mistress, a cancan dancer, her name I forgot. He would wait for her in front of the club, they'd take a carriage and visit a few more places before going back to their hotel. There, Uncle Ernő would be treated to a command performance. Because this woman had a specialty for which she was very famous. Do you know what kind of dance the cancan is?" He let go of my head, stood up, hummed some tune, and threw his legs up really high. He stopped, catching his breath. "Like that! Tremendous! Well, this woman was famous for being able not only to kick higher than anybody else but, with every beat as she kicked, to let go of a big one." At first I didn't understand. He threw himself down on my bed. We were slapping and grabbing at each other, we were laughing so hard. And I imagined the woman raising her legs and doing it with every kick. And he stayed like that, his body across mine, the way he'd been when he was laughing, but he wasn't laughing any more. Then he got up and left. In the morning I awoke to find his face clean-shaven, and he smelled like the rest of us. But when I opened my eyes I didn't know whether I had dreamed that or not. I went out into the garden. It had rained during the night. Lots of peaches were lying on the ground under the tree. Grandmama stayed in bed all day. Lying down she wouldn't be dizzy and her head wouldn't ache. She put the candy under her pillow, but she wouldn't always give me any. When I said I was hungry, she'd spread some fat or mustard on a slice of bread. I went out to eat in the garden. At night, if I woke up, I'd see her standing by the window. In the evening, after Grandpapa's death, she turned off the lights because she didn't like to waste electricity. She sat down on my bed. I asked her to keep her promise and tell me the story of Genaéva. "On the cover of this book, the book was my father's, was a big angel about to fly up to heaven, and this angel was Genaéva, and when husking corn or just sitting around with nothing to do in winter, my father liked me to read this legend out loud. It began like this: Once upon a time there lived a fabulously beautiful girl, no one had ever seen such a beauty before, ever; her golden hair reached down to her waist, and when she ran, the wind would catch the golden hair and make it fly all around her, but the girl was poor and her parents old. And the old parents died and poor Genaéva was left all alone. One day a young prince rode by. Genaéva happened to be in the forest where she had gone to collect twigs to cook some soup for herself in the evening. That's where he laid eyes on her. And immediately fell in love. He promised to marry her if she went along with him. But Genaéva did not want to, because she said it couldn't be, the rich prince couldn't be the husband of a poor girl. The prince grew angry and decided he would take her by force. Genaéva had barely got home when the prince's henchmen came for her. She was taken to a magnificent palace, where they bathed her in rosewater, dressed her in velvet, and her golden hair was braided with precious jewels. That's how she was led before the prince. Now do you believe that I love you, Genaéva? asked the prince. But Genaéva answered, How could I? She would believe it only if the prince would come home with her, to her little hut, eat onion soup for supper and during the day till the land. That's all the prince needed to hear. He immediately left the palace and went with her. But he could not put up with his new life for long. The oven smoke irritated his delicate eyes, the smell of onion stung his nose, and his soft palms could not hold the plow handles. One day the old king heard that his son was wasting away because of his love. He sent masked servants, who took Genaéva away and threw her into a dungeon. And the old king was happy to press his son to his breast. He told the prince that Genaéva had been abducted by robbers, and now the young prince had no choice but to marry the elegant countess with refined manners whom his father had chosen for him. And that's just what happened, and Genaéva gave birth to her son in the dungeon. One night, while the guard was snoring, Genaéva escaped. She hid in the forest, living on crab apples, wild cherries, and raw mushrooms, and then found shelter in a cave. That's how the two of them lived as the little boy was growing up. Genaéva's long hair was their cover, and soft green moss their bed. But one day Genaéva fell ill. She was so sick she couldn't move. Then a huge rain came from the skies. To get out of the rain, a family of deer sought refuge in the cave, and the hind, the mother deer, heard a little child crying. She suckled him. From then on, they all lived together as one big family, Genaéva, the deer, and the little boy. Until one day the peace of the forest was disturbed by the noise of humans and of other animals. Dogs came barking and yelping, horses were snorting. The deer fled. The good-hearted hind was brought low in front of the cave by the prince's weapon. The hind wept and the sound brought a little boy toddling out of the cave; he was crying, too. The hunting party couldn't have been more amazed. The prince jumped off his horse and went into the cave, where he found Genaéva, whose soul was just being released from the earth by angels. And the prince cried and cried, but in vain. Genaéva's soul was rising heavenward and had time only to say,

Raise him! That child is your son! These were her last words. Whenever I read this story in our house, everybody cried. We got the book from the priest. Yes, my father cried, too. And now I'll tell you my secret. Are you asleep?"

It's coming from behind. There's lots of it because it's floating, it's spreading in all directions, it's everywhere, as it flows it fills up everything; black, soft, shapeless, coming from behind. It pushes my head forward. It's everywhere now, a body. And it has pushed my head so far forward that I can't turn. I opened my eyes. The soft, shapeless something has slipped away, back behind my head. My bed. But it's here, around my bed. No use thinking I dreamed it all, it's waiting, here, behind my back. I closed my eyes, so as not to see the bed, the room. It swims around my head, softly. It's black. I pressed my face to the pillow. I couldn't move. And it seeped in, under my eyelids. I sat up quickly, which pushed the soft black thing back. This is my bed. This is my room. Again it is waiting—about my head, behind my back—but if I don't close my eyes it can't come closer. Outside, the moon was shining and pressed the dark shadows of the trees into the room. I got up to see whether it was in the garden. White dahlias in the shadows of the trees. As if the white dahlias were telling me where it was. White showing in the darkness. The door was open. Grandmama wasn't standing by the window of her room. Grandpapa's bed was empty. I couldn't see Grandmama's bed from here because that part of the room was very dark. Carefully I started for her bed to see if she was asleep. The floor creaked a little. "Is that you?" Grandmama asked from the darkness. "Yes." "Don't turn on the light!" Grandmama said softly from the darkness. She seemed to speak from a place farther away than her bed. "Aren't you feeling well? Grandmama, aren't you feeling well, Grandmama?" Her face on the pillow turned toward me softly. "A little. Just a little." Her hand moved on the cover, but did not reach toward me. I bent over her, to see her. "Go back to bed, child. Go to sleep." On the night table I groped for the light switch and my hand knocked against a glass, and I thought Grandpapa's teeth were in the glass. "No! Don't turn it on! I don't want you to see it. It's ugly."

I found the switch anyway. Only water in the glass. Now I was completely awake and knew where I was in my own life. Grandpapa was dead. Grandmama was looking at me. I didn't see anything ugly. As if surprised by something, she opened her eyes even wider and kept on looking at me. I waited, for she seemed about to ask me something, but she didn't. It could be only the stripes on my pajamas. She wasn't looking into my eyes but at my neck, and I touched my neck, maybe there was something there. Then a smile spread over her face, as if to say how silly I was and didn't even know what was happening; but her eyes didn't move, only the wrinkles around her mouth, as if she were smiling again. "Grandmama!" She kept looking. Didn't answer. Her mouth opened nice and slow and I could see she wasn't smiling. There was a scream. And then silence. But there was nobody behind me. And then something did happen, after all. I heard silence coming out of her body. But not all of the silence, because it kept coming out of her body. I am standing here in the silence that's coming out of her body, through her mouth, and also through her hands. I can't budge it, it can't be moved. That's what Grandmama had said! The eyelids must be held down now, the chin tied up, because it's cooling off. As if she were opening her eyes even wider, but no, only to me does it seem that way. For her, everything was the same. I didn't want her to look at me any more. I tried, as Grandmama had tried with Grandpapa; I was holding them down with my finger, to make them stay, like Grandpapa's; the lamp shone behind the teeth and I could tell she wasn't empty inside, as Grandpapa had been. The kerchief was there, on the chair, the kerchief Grandmama wears at home, but when she goes out she sometimes puts on a hat, too, because she's almost completely bald. Her skin feels warm in my hand. Her teeth still stuck out a little, with my finger I adjusted her mouth, too; maybe that's what she meant when she said, It's ugly. I turned off the light. In the dark I sat in Grandpapa's armchair. After I sat there a long time the room grew light because the moon was shining outside, and I could see Grandmama lying motionless, my eyes got used to the dark. I would have liked to cry, but I didn't let myself because I was waiting for something that might still happen, though I didn't know what. And then I remembered that Grandmama had once told me that a white wall serpent lived in every house and it comes out of the wall wherever somebody dies. I knew it was only a tale, but I pulled up my feet just in case it was true. When I woke up I thought it was a dream, but I was sitting in the armchair and outside it was getting light, and the birds! and I was cold in the armchair, and Grandmama was lying there with the kerchief on her face, the one I'd tied up on top of her head while there was still time. I listened to her and it seemed that all the silence had come out of her and there was none left. And maybe it was my fault, because of the kerchief! shouldn't have tied the kerchief while she was still alive! I untied the kerchief, her mouth didn't open. But even so, she wasn't alive. In the morning I heard the garbage cart. A horse was pulling the cart, the man was walking alongside and ringing a bell for people to bring out their garbage. I watched him from the window. He didn't stop at our house when he saw that nobody was going to come out. Then I went back to Grandmama and she was still lying the same way, and I cried because I didn't know what I was supposed to do. When I wiped my eyes I thought that maybe it was all in my imagination. But Grandmama was still lying there, the same way. I went out to the street, maybe somebody would come by. When the garbage man comes tomorrow I'll talk to him. Or maybe in the market, to the woman with the dyed blond hair, though Grandmama didn't like her. No point going to school, it would be empty now. Or maybe to the man in church, the one who looked at us, at the elevation of the Host, and who consoled the blond woman behind the counter. But I can't go like this, in my pajamas, and I can't leave Grandmama alone. In the kitchen I poured water in the biggest pot and put it on the range to heat it up. On the top shelf in the kitchen there was flour, semolina, bread crumbs, and sugar, but I couldn't find the black powder. I also found a candle and a sausage wrapped in paper. Grandmama always hid the sausage. I lit the candle at Grandmama's head, closed the shutters, but I couldn't reach the mirror over the commode, and the kerchief slid down. The water was steaming in the kitchen. First I cut off only a small piece of sausage, but I ate it quickly and cut another piece. When I wanted to cut another piece, the knife slipped into my finger. I could see inside my flesh. But the blood bubbled out and trickled across my hand and dripped onto the plate, too. I held my finger high, got off the chair to go into the bathroom. But I didn't fall, only my head was getting closer to the stone, and the door opened, and the floor tiles tumbled down. Black-and-white. Just like the tiles in the kitchen. Gray, sinking into something very soft. The screaming can't be heard any more. It's all nice and cold. They seemed to be taking me somewhere, everything is fluttering and everything I'm wearing is white, but where am I? Somewhere. A car stopped by our gate, but nobody got out and the engine kept running. The garbage man didn't show up the next day. I wanted to dig a hole, but it was raining. Three men got out of the car. That's where I buried the dog, too. One of them stayed at the gate. Two men came along the path between the roses. Maybe they won't take me away. They wanted to ring the bell, but I opened the door before they could. "Anybody else home besides you, kid?" "Grandmama! My grandmama is dead!" "You don't say! And is there anybody else at home?" "No. Just me." All the doors were open. He told me to stand in front of the mirror. I did, and he stayed in the hallway, too, leaning against the door. And I thought, How interesting, now he can see me not only from the front but also from the back. The other man went inside. Now he's going into my room. Walking from open door to open door. He stops in Grandmama's room. "Béla! Come quick!" "What's up?" "Béla! Hurry up! We've got a body here, really!" They told me to stay there, not to be afraid, they'd be right back. But it wasn't they who came back but two other men in black, and they took Grandmama away. And they said to stay at home, somebody would come for me, and did I have food in the house? I didn't dare ask them to tell my father, because I knew. But next day nobody came. I took the garbage out, in case the garbage man came. In the morning he came and took it away as usual. I took the candy from under Grandmama's pillow. Stuck together. Bits of the paper bag on the candy. I kept sucking the candy, had to spit out the paper. When I bit down, the delicious filling squished out on my tongue. Black figures were running around in front of the window. They didn't know their heads would fit through the railing. When I woke in the middle of the night, they were knocking on the window. I thought there were many of them, but it was only one person. But not him. I got up carefully; the floor didn't creak until the hallway. The bell rang, but I didn't make a move. If the bell rings it's not him, because he always knocks. If I just stand here, without moving, whoever it is will go away, because they'll think they've already taken me away somewhere, and then secretly I'd stay. And then Father would come. The bell rang again, and the house really didn't like the ringing. I thought I couldn't hold out any more. But I couldn't get myself to open the door, either. In the mirror I could see my shadow, as if I were standing behind myself. "Father?" I asked very softly so only he could hear, if it was him. And though he rang again, I did think it was him. "Father, is that you?" "Open up, kid! I've come for you! Come on! Open up, don't be afraid!" The man told me to get dressed quickly because we're going to Mikosdpuszta and he has to get back. While I was getting dressed he turned on all the lights, I kept an eye on him so he wouldn't steal anything. "Is there an upstairs floor?" "Yes." "Rooms up there, too?" "Yes." "How many?" "Two." I put on my old sandals even though the new ones had rubber soles and the old ones pinched my foot. And he said I didn't have to take anything with me, because I'd have everything I needed there. But I still wanted to take something. While he was turning off the lights I slipped a pebble into my pocket. I had found this pebble in the garden when I wanted to dig the hole to bury Grandmama. I wanted the magnifying glass, too, but for that I didn't have time. He locked the door, but didn't give me back the key. "The gate has no key?" "Yes, it does, it hangs on a nail inside!" "Doesn't matter, somebody'll be coming here tomorrow, anyway." I didn't dare ask who. Big black car. He told me to sit in the back. There were curtains on the windows. I wanted to pull them aside, but he told me to leave them. We were going fast. He didn't talk to me. I was cold, it would have been nice to go back for a sweater. When I fell asleep I heard music. Once in a while he lit a cigarette. A small lamp was shining within the radio. I never rode so fast in a car before. The highway was completely empty. I saw the sun come up. It was all so strange, and I was glad to be traveling like this, but I had to say something because I couldn't hold it any more. "I've got to pee." But he wasn't angry. I got out and there was this huge meadow, the wind was blowing a little, I felt cold, but the sun was warming me up a little. I recognized all the birds—the larks!—and red poppies everywhere. If I started running now he couldn't catch me, because the car couldn't go through the meadow, and I could get away. But the mountains were too far, past the meadow. Maybe they were the mountains Grandpapa had told me about. Later the man said, We're almost there. We drove into the woods and it was cool again. And when we got through the woods I saw a castle on top of a hill, a big lake under it, and a stream flowing into the lake. The car rumbled over a bridge, we stopped in front of an iron gate. Two children opened the iron gate and we drove up a curving road to the front of the castle. The pebble road was popping under the big car. I could see the lake from here. Another man was standing in front of the castle and he opened the car door for me. A whistle on a red braid hung from his neck. "I'm turning right around," said the man who'd brought me. "Don't you want breakfast?" "No. I've got to get back by noon. Thank you." This other man got hold of my neck. Then the car disappeared in the forest. We were going upstairs on wide steps. He was holding me by my neck. We walked through a corridor, he opened a door and said I should wait in there, they'd be coming for me. He closed the door. I heard the sound of his footsteps, but he didn't go back where we'd come from but continued on in the other direction. This was a big room. The sun was shining in the windows, which had white curtains. Double bunks in the room. Black-and-white square tiles on the floor, just like our kitchen and bathroom. I stood by the door and was afraid to move, though I would have liked to look out the window. It was quiet, as if the whole place were empty. Five beds on one side, by the window, and five on the other side. White iron beds. Opposite the door a table, two chairs; white cloth on the table, a pitcher with water in it and two glasses on a tray. I kept listening, maybe I'd hear something, but there was no noise of any kind from anywhere. I started for the table and noticed that in the small lockers between the beds there were round holes, five holes in each locker. And the windows were open. Now and then the wind would nudge the curtains, and just as the curtains moved so did the shadows on the floor. The two chairs stood at the same angle at either end of the table. I didn't sit down. Somewhere downstairs, far away, dishes were clattering. That must be breakfast. And I also smelled a strange smell. From the window I saw the pebbled area in front of the castle where the car had brought me; it was interesting to look at it from above. And a white swan was swimming on the lake toward the bridge. But I couldn't go on looking because I thought I heard somebody coming. The doorknob didn't move. Only clattering sounds from somewhere downstairs, from far away. I started walking, stepping only on the white squares. Sometimes the tips of my sandals slipped over the line onto a black square, even though the rule was that I could step only on the white ones. When I reached the door the rule changed: I was allowed to step only on the black squares, all the way back to the table. The glasses were dry. I wanted to pour, but I missed a little and the tablecloth got wet. The door opened behind my back. And I hadn't even heard any steps. Blue sneakers on his feet. A very tall boy. Didn't say anything, just looked at me. And he lowered his head. The sun was shining brightly just then. His wavy blond hair fell on his forehead and sparkled. He held the doorknob. Then he pulled the door shut. He spoke in a whisper: "You are Péter Simon?" When he asked this, he lazily threw back his head and his hair flew off his forehead and he looked at me again; even like that his hair sparkled above his forehead. "Yes." His forehead was high and curved and smooth, and I would have liked him to come over to me right then. He kept standing by the door. He whispered again: "Come on." I started toward him. The squares were moving under my feet, every which way, black ones and white ones, and that was good, though it bothered me a little that I wasn't stepping on the black and white squares according to the rule; I don't know why, I also felt that I was a little afraid of him. "Well! Come on, then!" He again lowered his head and his hair fell across his forehead. I was standing right in front of him. I could already smell him. Gray spots on his sneakers: mud. But I wanted to see his eyes. And then he pressed me to himself. His naked arms clasped my back. And I hugged him, too, and we just stood there like that. On his chest the undershirt was sweaty, almost wet, but it felt good, and I didn't want to move from there. My arms on his waist; the hard collision of bones and the warmth of his lap, and my face felt the arches of his ribs under the sweaty undershirt and I didn't want to move from there and I closed my eyes to feel him even more. He squeezed me. His voice came into me, behind my eyes. "Don't be afraid! Now we're going to see the principal, but there won't be any problem with her. Don't be afraid. All right? Don't ever be afraid of anything. All right? Never! Of anything!" He let go of me, but I still wanted to go on squeezing him so I could bury my face in the darkness. "Come on!" He stroked my face, a hard palm, and I had to open my eyes. "Come on." In the corridor we walked side by side, I didn't look at him, but felt him next to me, his soundless steps in his sneakers. He was only walking, but I had to hurry to keep up. I don't know which direction we were going, I just went wherever his steps were leading me. Then he stopped in front of an enormous brown door. He knocked. A voice called out something. He whispered, "Don't be afraid, I'll wait for you!" He opened the door, and I also felt he was the one who closed it after I stepped inside. A woman wearing glasses was sitting behind the desk. She was old. She motioned me to come closer. In the evening, before climbing up to my bed, I asked one of the boys, he had a dark face, who the boy was who had come for me. But the dark-faced boy didn't answer. For two days we weren't allowed to talk. There were boxes everywhere in the institution. Whoever talked had his name thrown into one of these boxes, by the daily monitors or by anybody else; any other violation of the rules also had to be reported this way. When we marched into the dining room I didn't know where I was supposed to sit. Long tables and benches. It was hard to climb behind the benches. Cocoa in polka-dotted mugs, then I didn't know that was to be breakfast every morning, and it was so hot we had to drink it slowly. But there was one empty place, that's where I sat. That was also the table where he sat, the dark-faced boy, whose name was János Angyal. When the two days of silence were over, after lights-out he called me down to his bunk, because he was sleeping under me, and said he was born in France, that's why he was here, and he would tell me all about it, but now he wanted me to tell him something. But I couldn't think of anything. Because I felt it wouldn't be a good idea to ask again about that other boy. One had to be careful not to be informed on in one of the boxes; those who had complaints written against them had to report to Comrade Dezső. A whistle hung from Comrade Dezső's neck. When the whistle was heard everybody ran to stand by their beds and Comrade Dezső came with the two big boys who committed the crime against him and the lockers were thoroughly searched. I got clothes, and sneakers, blue ones, another pair of shoes, a toothbrush, soap, and a towel. In the dining room on a huge tray a pile of buttered bread. When Comrade Dezső blew the whistle we could sit down and everyone would try to get the bigger slices, everyone was allowed to have two. The big slices could be folded in two and put inside your shirt, and in the evening, after lights-out, friends could share them. Angyal even had some salt. After lights-out friends would go over to one another's beds. But when there was an alert they would catch this, and also find the buttered bread in lockers or under the mattresses. Anybody caught with buttered bread would get no cocoa the next morning. In the morning we ran naked to physical training. Everybody was embarrassed because that's when the women were coming to work in the kitchen. After the exercise we went running and never knew if we'd go bathing in the lake or not. When we were allowed to, Comrade Dezső would yell: "To the lake! On the run! Not yet, that was no signal! On the run! What is it with you? That was no signal, I said! On the run! Now!" When he blew the whistle we ran. When he blew it again we had to come out of the water. They were watching us very closely because the last one out couldn't go to the lake the next day. That's why all we did was splash one another at the edge of the lake. In the morning, at the lake, all the groups were together. Vilmos Merényi always swam in the lake, alone. Comrade Dezső laughed because somebody always had to be last. But he didn't count Merényi. Merényi climbed out by the bridge and ran back to us from there. I noticed that on one of his thighs he had a thick vein with lots of little branches. Friday, after house cleaning, we went to shower. But starting with Saturday morning we were not to talk or make any sound until Monday morning. We took soap and towels to the bathroom. Angyal said the big boys were doing something in the showers, but I didn't understand what. Once, I said my stomach hurt; when it was the big boys' turn to go, I told Comrade Dezső that my stomach didn't hurt any more, and he let me go with the big boys. The big boys could stand under the showers longest, until all the hot water was used up, because they were the last to shower. But they didn't do anything, Angyal had lied, they only looked at one another. By then Vilmos had gone. One day something happened. We marched down to the dining room and the teachers left. First there was only quiet. The teachers didn't come back. Then the big boys began to horse around under the piano. Only the big ones. Vilmos was also there, and I was watching him. When he crawled out he saw I was watching him and he waved to me. Angyal was my friend, but I didn't tell him I would have liked Vilmos Merényi for my best friend more. I was afraid Angyal might notice this waving. Whenever friends had a fight they would inform on each other in one of the boxes. That day the principal also came into the dining room. We never saw her, even the corridor leading to her office you could enter only with special permission. When I came out through the brown door he wasn't there any more, and all the time I'd been in the office all I thought about was how he was waiting for me. The principal's hair was as if she had never combed it. She was sitting in a white smock, and here too the curtains were white. Her glasses slipped down, she pushed them back; she signaled that I should come closer. I felt the thick carpet under my feet, like the one in Grandpa-pa's room, and it would have been nice to see if it had the same patterns. "Sit down, my son, let's have a little chat." The chair felt cool. The sun shone through the white curtains and I couldn't see her face too well, or her eyes behind the glasses. I felt as if I were in the middle of some huge whiteness and out of the light a voice was coming toward me. "First of all I'd like to welcome you on my behalf and on behalf of the entire collective of this institution." It was as if she wasn't moving her mouth while she talked. She was whispering. "You must be tired, you probably didn't get any sleep, poor thing. But you'll get plenty of rest. In a few days everything will be all right. I hope you'll like it here. Our strength will make you strong. Here you'll become a hardy and resolute individual. Are you sleepy? Maybe we should talk tomorrow?" "No." "Well, all right, then. In a word, your new life will begin here. To become a useful member of the collective, as if you were born just now, your new life will have to cover over your old life, so that you can become a new man! Here, in our place, democracy rules. That is why no matter what you think or feel you can tell me or anyone else. And not as if to an adult: when you talk to me you are talking to an equal member of our community. Here we don't talk baby-talk, do you understand?" "Yes." She spoke gently, the light made her gray hair glitter, and I was ashamed for having to blink all the time. "Getting down to the matter." She took off her glasses and I could see her eyes. Blue. "Those who will be your friends here have had fates similar to yours. The burden of the parents' crimes must be cast off. In this, we, your more mature mates, will be of considerable help to you. What exactly are we talking about?" The eyes once again disappeared behind the flashing glasses. She got up, came over to me, and laid her hands on my shoulders. She held me firm and shook me a little. I didn't dare close my eyes. "The man you've called your father until now is not your father. His crime has made him unworthy of fatherhood. You probably don't know what I'm talking about yet, do you?" "Traitor," I said softly. Her palms gripped my shoulders, her face trembled, and I saw behind the glasses that she was starting to cry. Her mouth and eyebrows were twitching in all directions, and I saw that no matter how hard she tried she couldn't control them; only her palms went on squeezing my shoulders. "Dear God!" Her tears trickled out from below the thin gold rim of her glasses. "Yes."

She whispered: "He betrayed you, too." She took off her glasses, and turning away to the window, she wiped her eyes with her fist. "Excuse me. I got a bit emotional. Though I mustn't. And you must forget you saw me like this." She drew the curtain aside and looked out. The light shone through her white smock. She was smiling when she turned back toward me. "Come here!" She put her arm around my shoulders and we looked out the window. Down in the courtyard they were lining up in columns. Heads. In white undershirts and blue sweatpants, like the boy waiting for me outside the door. The columns filled the whole yard. In nice orderly rows they stood, in straight lines one behind the other, without moving. The white stripes of the undershirts over the tanned shoulders. On a tall pole the flag, and the breeze was making the flag flutter a little. The sun was shining. I waited for somebody to look up and see that I was there. They were all looking straight ahead. "Now, even among us, crime has reared its ugly head." She was whispering: "Hideous, terrible crime. We have ordered complete silence for two days so that everyone could search his own soul and think about what has happened. When you leave this office, go over there, see? There, in the third row of the fourth column we left a place empty for you! Starting with this moment, for two days you're not allowed to say anything to anyone, and nobody's allowed to talk to you, either. And now you have to go!" Not in front of the door, not in the corridor, not anywhere. The boy wasn't waiting for me. In the courtyard I didn't find my place for a long time. It wasn't nice to hear the crunching pebbles in the big silence. And then I was standing there, too, with the rest of them. The sun was shining. The boy next to me flexed his knees and then straightened them again. He kept doing that. I stood straight, but later felt I had to do it, too, because I was getting tired and couldn't stand still all the time. The one in front of me was doing the same thing. But from somewhere above us we heard a whistle. "We are not moving, are we?" somebody yelled from above. But the boy in front of me still bent his knees once in a while, and so did the boy next to me. From where I stood I couldn't see the blond boy. The old sandals pinched my feet. The new ones with the rubber soles were in my locker. Somebody must have gone back to the house, because the tomorrow of then was already today. We ran around the courtyard. I didn't know where I was supposed to sit. The boy next to me hid a slice of buttered bread under his shirt. When nobody was looking some boys hissed. Somebody put a hand on my neck. The man who took me to the room. We were walking along a different corridor, down steps. He opened the door to another room. It was dark there. He turned on the light and gave me a pair of sneakers, blue ones, a pair of regular shoes, undershirt, underpants, sweatsuit, soap, toothbrush, and a towel. He wrote things in a book. He held on to my neck and we went upstairs. We walked into a room. I felt it wasn't the same room I'd been in before, but it was very much like that one. He opened the locker, one with five holes, and showed me where I should put everything. But he didn't say anything. Then he put his hand on the upper bunk and gave it a slap. He got hold of my neck again and we were on our way. We crossed the same courtyard and walked into a church. But inside it wasn't like our church. I didn't see any decorations, and in place of the altar, on a long platform, was a table covered with a red tablecloth. Everybody was already waiting, and my place was left empty. And then I was standing there with them. If I tilted my head just a little, I could make out underneath the white paint small patches of colored pictures, like stains. And high up, in the narrow windows, the light was coming through the stained glass. I thought of the window in our attic. We heard the door being shut, but nobody moved, only some of the boys locked and unlocked their knees; me too. From here I could see his hair, but I wasn't sure it was him. I thought of rolling around in the grass with my dog. The iron gate was opened. And we were running, our feet rumbling on the bridge, and the swans swam out on the lake. In a clearing we sat down and the man who had held my neck sat in the middle, and everybody could look wherever he wanted to. Only speaking was forbidden. I didn't feel like eating my lunch; I kicked the boy next to me and he quickly took my meat and put it on his own plate. He hissed. In the evening he was lying on the lower bunk, and before I climbed up to mine I asked him for the name of the blond boy who had come for me and sat opposite us in the clearing. But this boy didn't answer me. When I woke up I had to cover my eyes. The lights were on and I didn't know where I was. We were standing by our bunks. Everything had been thrown out of my locker, all over the floor, and I had to put it all back, make everything more orderly than before. In the morning they raised the flag, but we didn't go to the church or to the clearing. After lunch we stayed in the dining room. There was a piano there, too. With a lock on its lid. Until suppertime everybody had to sit there in his place. After supper we stood like that in the church, everybody in his place; the door opened and they were coming. Between the rows. But nobody looked, only straight ahead. The principal was in the lead, the man who had held my neck followed her, and after them came the rest of the teachers. They got to the platform and stood behind the table. The principal took off her glasses and looked at the man who came in behind her. And then the man yelled, "At ease!" But then he had to cough. Now everybody could do anything they wanted to with their knees. The principal waved her hand and the rest of the teachers sat down, but the principal remained standing and put her glasses back on. She raised her head. I wanted to look at the lamps, to see if they were giving enough light. "We have been silent for two days. The words, the human voice now probably sounds strange, surprising, to all of us." She stretched her hand toward us and her glasses glittered and this made her look as if she was angry with us, though she was talking very softly. "The reason we ordered the period of silence was precisely for this, that what is about to happen now should be memorable for everyone. Please bring up the two pupils from the cellar." Two teachers got up from the table and left, walking quickly between the ranks. While we were waiting, the principal took off and put back her glasses several times and remained standing. The man was coughing. And then they were coming in again from behind our backs, forward. I was afraid it might be him! that he'd been in the cellar! but it was two other boys, their hands tied with rope behind their backs. They went up on the platform and made the two boys turn to face us; both boys spread their legs a little, I don't know why. One of them raised his head high, but closed his eyes. The other one, as if looking for somebody among the rows, kept moving his eyes without settling anywhere. The teachers fidgeted, making their chairs creak. The principal stretched her arm in front of the two boys, but waited for complete silence, for the chairs to stop creaking. "Behold! The two criminals whose conscience is burdened with a crime for which they could be sentenced to death by hanging. But I don't wish to talk of it. My indignation is as great as my disgust. Let the person against whom the crime was committed speak now. I call on Comrade Dezső." The one who had held my neck. He stood up. Around his neck, on the braid, the whistle. He shouted, "Vilmos Merényi, step out and come forward!" Merényi went past me, drawing a little wind after him. With his head bowed, he was walking very slowly. He stopped before the other two and lazily tossed back his head to keep his wavy hair out of his forehead. "There you have it! Here they are! Now you can see the three bad apples all together! But you others, lying low in the protection of the ranks, don't delude yourself that . . . No! I won't let it! I won't let myself be carried away! Just look at this trash! Suhajda has closed his eyes! The virgin! Rat! He doesn't dare look his friends in the eye! The other one is trembling. Making in his pants! don't you dare smile! Only Merényi seems calm. Naturally. He thinks that everything has been settled as far as he's concerned. In fact, he's the most disgusting of them all! But I won't let this lowlife make me lose my temper! We have overcome our emotions, if any emotions were ever involved! Stick to the facts, we must always stick to the facts, and you can all see how calmly and reasonably I will present the horrible facts—before you hear the final decision of the teaching staff. Now then! Friday morning Merényi came to me and told me that Suhajda and Stark had asked him to steal a big knife from the kitchen. Which he did. Is that correct, Merényi?" "Yes." "Their intention was, since they knew that I never lock my door and that from the monitor's table one can see when I return to my room, at the appropriate time, that is to say, Friday night, to charge into my room and kill me with the knife. I told Merényi Friday morning, Go ahead! And Merényi agreed to help set the trap. And this is how it happened! On Friday, Stark was the monitor on duty. He was sitting opposite my room, hiding the knife in the drawer of the monitor's table. Suhajda stole out into the garden, watching to see when I turned off my light. I turned off my light at 9:25. As agreed, they waited another half hour. Merényi, who was standing guard by the main staircase, gave the signal that the coast was clear. Is that how it was? Suhajda!" "Yes." "So then, at ten o'clock Suhajda checked the window one more time and came up from the garden, Stark took the knife out of the drawer and turned off the lights in the corridor. Stark!" "Yes." "Merényi gave another all-clear signal. Then these two approached my room, silently, Suhajda suddenly tore open the door, and in one leap Stark was at my bedside! and stuck the knife into me. He would have, that is, if I hadn't been sitting in the armchair. In that very instant I blinded them with my flashlight. The evidence is still there, the knife slashed through my quilt. And I yelled, Hands up! You can see how calmly I've related this bloody story. And now I want everyone to know the teaching staff's decision. We will not hand the conspirators over to the police. They will stay here among us. We will not shirk our responsibility. We are here to extirpate the crimes that try to infiltrate our ranks, and we most certainly shall! Suhajda and Stark will remain members of the collective. Even though they attempted to commit the most heinous crime? Yes. Their greatest punishment is that I am alive and that they will not die, or go on living, as self-glorified heroes. At the same time we cannot deny them a certain amount of admiration. They were brave, but since they put their bravery in the service of a horrendous crime, let them suffer for it. Have no fear, I personally guarantee that they will suffer. Merényi, however, is a traitor! It is to his credit, let it be said, that he betrayed his partners for a good cause, but he did so not out of honesty but out of base cowardice. That is why the teaching staff has decided that he, too, will remain here, but he cannot be a member of the collective and we expel him from our ranks. We have drawn the proper conclusions from these events. One: we shall tighten the regulations of our institution so that crime will never be able to rear its head again.

And two: to prevent such despicable, cowardly betrayal from ever recurring, we shall place boxes at various points of the corridor; anyone who has anything to say, or to complain about, should write it down and put the paper into one of the boxes. And to memorialize this terrible affair properly, I hereby order the transfer of general cleaning day from Saturday to Friday; if on Friday the external filth is removed, then on Saturday we may begin to get rid of the internal filth. Between reveille on Saturday morning and reveille on Monday complete silence will rule the entire institution! There! That means now! After fall-out. No talking after fall-out, either! That means everybody. Everybody has heard what I've said, and remember, from now until tomorrow morning. Until tomorrow morning everybody has time to come to the right conclusions. And now, team! 'Ten-shun! At ease! And now, by groups, the whole team will march out." When we marched out on Saturday afternoon, the bridge rumbled and the swans swam out on the lake. We could also see them from the windows. Before dark they'd swim back under the bridge. The heat had already been turned on, but at night we weren't allowed to close the windows. When the grass was wet we would just stand around the clearing, Comrade Dezső would go for a walk. The leaves were falling nicely. When one day we marched into the dining room and the teachers had gone off somewhere and the big boys were horsing around under the piano, Merényi crawled out from under the piano and waved to me. And then the principal came downstairs, too. She said the institution would be dissolved because it had accomplished its mission, and everybody would be sent to some other place. But nothing happened. Once in a while a new child would arrive. In the morning we didn't have to run out naked any more, morning exercises were held in the chapel, because it started to snow. Comrade Dezső promised we'd get sleds and skis and then we'd go on a big excursion. One day, after lights-out, Merényi stuck his head in and waved to me to come out. Angyal also saw this. I went out to the corridor, I was already in my pajamas, Merényi was still dressed. He said his train was leaving that evening, he was going to the Rákóczi, the military academy, and if they let him out he would come to see me, and that I should go to the Rákóczi, too. I was afraid he'd hug me again, but we only shook hands, and then he walked away in the corridor. When I got back, Angyal didn't ask what Merényi had wanted. It occurred to me that he might inform on me, but he didn't; that's why he stayed my friend. But one morning after reveille, Comrade Dezső came in and said that as of today Hőgyész and Angyal would change places. So Hőgyész got the lower bunk and Angyal got an upper bunk near the window, right opposite mine. And of course I couldn't go to him there after lights-out. I thought this happened because of Merényi, anyway, because we talked in the corridor. Hőgyész is the dumbest one in the whole group, that's why I didn't feel like calling him to me or going down to visit him. And I didn't want to be seen with him, because I felt that Angyal was still my friend. But I will go to a military academy. On Saturday and Sunday it was always quiet, nobody talked. If we still had something to say, we'd hiss. The swans have a little house on the lakeshore in case the lake freezes over. We got only two skis from the army, white ones to match the terrain. Comrade Dezső went skiing with Suhajda on Saturday. I remembered how stupidly we had argued about who would sit in front on the sled. The Mama always sat in front, the child in the middle, and the Papa was steering in the rear. But we liked Comrade Dezső anyway. Whenever there was an alert at night, we thought the time had come to dissolve the institution. If Suhajda and Stark flung everything out of the lockers and they weren't right, Comrade Dezső chewed them out for being bullies. He was fair. There weren't enough showers and we had to push and shove one another, and we could scream all we wanted. This time Angyal didn't ask me to scrub his back. One morning, before breakfast, somebody was screaming. Sat up in his bunk and just kept screaming. Everybody woke up. I'd been just dreaming that a kitten had fallen into the sewage canal and the rest of the kittens, running after it, all fell in; the canal was very deep and the mother cat wanted to go after them, but the ladder going down was made of steel, nothing to hold on to with her claws, and she fell into the dirty water, too. It was still dark outside, very early in the morning. Kolozsvári was sitting up in his bunk screaming and screaming. And then everybody was screaming. They were all jumping up and down on top of the beds and somebody started to throw pillows all over the place. It wasn't me. And all the while everybody was screaming as hard as they could. Pillows were flying. And then I saw that Angyal was on his knees on his bunk and screamed and took aim with his pillow and screamed; he got me right in the face. And I was glad he was still my friend and still loved me. I screamed, too. Picked up the pillow and yelled and jumped up on my bed, and the bed sent me up and up, it had good springs, and I was screaming all the time, and took aim and with all my might threw the pillow back at him. Smack into his mug! The pillow was flying, my foot got caught on something hard, Angyal ducked and the pillow flew right out the window, ouuuuut! the stone floor is hurtling into me, black, white. Scintillation all about me. Then darkness. And the screaming is approaching, receding. Somewhere the door opened, and gray as if in something very soft in this white one right in the middle. Nice and cold. Cracking. Empty snail shell. "Can you hear me over here!" Soft roots, dark, can't go any deeper, can't see out any more. Can not.